WOMAN OF BLOOD & BONE

Rogue Ethereal Series - Book 1

ANNIE ANDERSON

WOMAN OF BLOOD & BONE
Rogue Ethereal Book 1

International Bestselling Author
Annie Anderson

Edited by Angela Sanders
Cover Design by Danielle Fine
Formatted by Tattered Quill Designs

www.annieande.com

For my other two amigas.

BOOKS BY ANNIE ANDERSON

PHOENIX RISING SERIES

Flame Kissed

Death Kissed

Fate Kissed

Shade Kissed

Sight Kissed

ROGUE ETHEREAL SERIES

Woman of Blood & Bone

Daughter of Souls & Silence

Lady of Madness & Moonlight

Sister of Embers & Echoes

Priestess of Storms & Stone

SHELTER ME SERIES

Seeking Sanctuary

Reaching Refuge

Chasing Cover

Seek You Find Me

(A Romantic Suspense Newsletter Serial)

CHAPTER ONE

MAX

I was burned at the stake when I was fourteen years old. At nineteen, I was dissected by a zealot "physician" who knew less than a pile of cow shit about medicine. I was drowned in a lake when I was twenty-four. At twenty-seven, I was stoned in a public square.

When I was thirty—long after I quit aging—I finally got smart. If I stopped helping people, if I stopped trying to save the humans who were so ungrateful for my assistance, no one would know what I could do. I wouldn't hear the word "witch" from the lips of men who didn't know the first thing about me.

Sure, it meant more people would die, but with as many times as I'd been "killed" for my gift, they deserved it.

I made rules—ways of hiding in plain sight.

One: never, ever, on literal pain of death, live in a small town. There is no hiding there, no way to keep nosy people out of your business. Also, when the town magistrate happens to go "missing," they are going to look at the strange girl who keeps to herself. Yes, I killed him, and no, I'm not sorry.

He deserved it.

Two: no matter how much I may want to, don't cast in public. It doesn't matter if some asshole parent is beating their kid, mistreating their dog, or driving like a blind monkey on uppers. Don't do it. Memory spells are slippery and difficult to execute.

Three: Don't talk about history or politics with people. You run the risk of talking about the French Revolution as if you were actually there (I was), and then some jerkoff history buff—who swears by the books he so ardently clings to—starts getting nosy. It's bad news all around.

I remind myself of my rules—*especially rule two*—as I walk the dark and rather dirty streets of Denver's warehouse district. While I suppose I could get scolded for being a beautiful woman walking alone at night in a big city in a decidedly seedy part of town, I just don't give a fuck. I wasn't leaving my cherry-red Chevelle anywhere but in a highly secure parking garage, even with the three-block walk on five-inch spiked heels. And I'd break rule two in a heartbeat if a man—or woman, I'm equal opportunity—came at me in this part of town. Like the shady-looking fellow giving me the "V" sign as he adjusts his crotch, his tongue waggling through his fingers like some sort of deranged animal.

I contemplate just what I could turn him into. A trash barrel, or maybe a port-a-john, or even a mailbox. Transmogrification spells aren't too hard if you're working with something of equal mass. All it would take is a snap of my fingers and the right words in Latin.

My plans are derailed by my phone ringing in my clutch. Lucky prick.

Someone just saved your life, pal.

I fish the slim, yet annoying device from the creamy pink satin of my bag and answer it.

"You just saved someone's life and ruined my fun. I hope you know I'm going to make the next tattoo I do on you hurt," I grouse, stomping my way down the cracked sidewalk toward my destination.

"No, you won't," Aurelia says, "and sweetheart, if you could make me feel pain, I'd lick your freaking pumps. Why are you planning murder?"

Aurelia Constantine has been one of my best friends for the better part of a century. We bonded over being cast out of our respective families and our mutual love of tattoos—me giving them, and Ari receiving them. Aurelia is a phoenix—like, no shit, flaming-wings-and-everything phoenix. I, on the other hand, am something altogether different.

"Some jackoff is making a rude gesture at me. Speaking of, what would be a worse fate? Life as a port-a-john or trashcan? I can see significant downsides to both," I muse, my fingertips itching to snap.

"Stop plotting the silly human's demise for a minute. Are you coming to my wedding or not, woman? You keep flip-flopping and I can't see what you're going to do." Aurelia is a rare and powerful psychic, and newly crowned leader, along with her twin, Mena of the American Phoenix Legion, and if she can't see what I'm going to decide, it really must be up in the air.

In all honesty, I can't see myself—a Rogue witch—hobnobbing with all of the powerful Ethereal leaders that will deign to be there. It sounds like a sure-fire way to get myself thrown in a dark hole somewhere to never be heard from again.

Yeah, I don't think so.

"I feel horrible, but I don't think I'm going to be able to make it, babe. It seems too risky. All it takes is one coven leader to be there, and then I'll be carted off to some dank hole in the ground praying to die. I really want to be there, but..." I trail off, unwilling to disappoint one of the few people who has made this long, lonely life somewhat bearable.

"I get it, sweetie. Don't beat yourself up. You still planning on coming to the bachelorette party? Evan is cooking up something weird and probably hilarious as hell."

Evangeline Carmichael, Queen Wraith and all-around pixie badass, is an odd duck but a hilarious one. Whatever she's planning for a bachelorette party is sure to be a smashing success.

"This, I can do. You swear you're not upset?" It isn't every day that one of your besties gets married—even though technically this is her second wedding, and she has been bound to her husband Rhys for the better part of two centuries.

"Darling girl, if there was anyone in this world who understood hiding out, it would be me. No worries. I'll see you in a few days."

"You're bringing the twins into the shop, right? I need to squeeze those little balls of baby goodness."

Aurelia's twins, Henry and Olivia, are a solid bright spot in my life. I can't wait to see them grow up. There isn't anything in the world I wouldn't do to keep them safe.

"Yes, if I can get Rhys to tone down the bodyguard detail. Oh, shit! I need to go, babe. Henry is hungry, and if Rhys picks him up, well..." She trails off. Her son Henry inherited some of the Constantine family traits. Namely the Aegis ability—one which shields and electrocutes anything within a ten-foot radius. I foresee his toddler years to be pure hell.

"Okay, babe. Have fun with that," I say as I disconnect, picking up the pace on my black suede peep-toes on the uneven sidewalk. If I wreck these shoes, I will murder Striker on principle.

Striker Voss is my business partner and other best friend. And his ignorant ass convinced me to get dressed up and meet him out here in the ass end of nowhere to get into an exclusive club. How Strike managed to get a plus-one, I'm not sure, and with his abilities, I probably don't want to know.

But here I am in what I think is the perfect club number—a royal-blue velvet, off-the-shoulder wiggle dress from the '50s. The gathered bust and tulip-style pencil skirt make it classy and racy. Plus, the three-quarter sleeves show off a hint of my tattoos—just enough to keep people guessing—and the blue of the dress compliments the freshly dyed indigo of my hair.

The nearly silent purr of the engine pulling up next to me yanks my eyes from my feet and my awareness from the man across the street. The whir of a window lowering is followed closely by Striker's low whistle. He pulls into a parking lot a hundred feet down the road, and exits his Tesla Roadster like he's a model strutting down a runway.

Striker is beautiful in a way that is almost unearthly.

Wavy blond, shoulder-length hair, cheekbones sharp enough to cut glass, a jaw dreams were made of, and a pair of lips I know for a fact are just as soft and yet just as firm as one would hope them to be. Eyelashes that would make a model weep brush his cheekbones as he blinks, and I swear, if I didn't already know we weren't compatible in bed, I would hold him hostage and drain him dry.

But I do know how incompatible we are. Margaritas plus an unfortunate anniversary, equaled a solid degeneration to straight tequila and a rather fumbling night together in the 1940s. Striker is a giver—given his species, it's understandable—but in bed, I need a taker. He couldn't be a taker if I held a gun to his head, thus, no more naughty times with Striker. It was awkward for about two seconds until we both laughed about it and moved the fuck on with our lives.

Living as long as we do, little things like sleeping with your best friend tend to get swept under the rug. What doesn't get swept away is the dick move of dragging me out into the middle of stab-central in a club dress.

"Yeah, I know I look good. Could you pretty please tell me why you dragged me out here? I almost turned a thug into a port-a-john for Fate's sake."

Typically, Striker is the one bitching about something, but tonight my back is sore from hunching over one body part or another, inking fresh designs on smooth skin. I love my shop, love my job, but nights like tonight, I'd rather soak in my garden tub and drink a big old glass of wine than go out to this club Strike's been raving about for the last five years.

"All in good time. I swore I would take you to the hottest club in town, but before we go in, there are rules."

Rules, my fabulous ass. What am I, nine?

"I'm nearly four hundred years old, Strike. Not, in fact, the teenager you are treating me as."

Striker gives me the raised eyebrow of impatience and carries on. "As I was saying. Let me open the door for you. Only members can access the building. Don't pay the bartender. Drinks are free and they work for tips only. Do not hand him money, put it in the tip jar. If he touches you, he'll know you're not a member and that is bad news all around. Try and stick to my booth when we get in, and for Fate's sake, do not go on the dance floor. It's like a Roman fucking orgy in there. I plan on sticking to you like glue, but if we get separated, be careful. I swear this place is pure shenanigans. It's like the witches took a look at Fae clubs and decided to go one bigger. Ugh. Like they can compete with Fae clubs."

This rigmarole tells me something hinky is going on. Wait a minute…

"You don't have a plus-one at all, do you? You're sneaking me in? Have you lost your damn mind?"

I may not have ever been to a witch club, but I know enough about them to know only accepted coven members are allowed admittance for one, and two, they have a rule about no Rogues. Striker assured me he could get me into the local club since he had an in.

"You know me, it's better to ask for forgiveness, blah, blah, blah. Just come on. Have I ever steered you wrong?" he asks as he pulls me by the elbow.

"Yes. Several times in the last century, fucker."

"Okay, but"—He pauses, opening the creaky warehouse door which seems to have appeared out of nowhere —"look at this place."

Striker is about to get me in a world of trouble, I just know it.

CHAPTER TWO

MAX

S triker pulls me one step into the warehouse, and the outside streets of Denver fall away, the door sealing shut behind us as if it were never there.

Well, that isn't creepy at all. If I were by myself, that little move would have me running for the door which is no longer there.

There isn't a doorman or entryway, just a vast, dark room, teeming with people dancing and drinking and laughing. Multicolored spotlights make intricate patterns on the black ceiling, seeming to shimmer and move of their own accord unlike any strobe light I've ever seen.

Elegant naked men and women are suspended from swaths of fabric, hanging from the ceiling and performing some sort of erotic acrobatic act above the dance floor. Beyond them is a large bar with shirtless bartenders of both sexes mixing drinks. Striker wasn't lying. This place is like one huge orgy.

"So noted," I murmur, and Striker laughs as he leads me through a throng of revelers to a red leather semicircular booth, tucked in a corner away from the loudest of the music. It's dark, lit only by the light of a small candle sitting on a slight stainless-steel table, but it has a great view of the dance floor and the pure unadulterated hedonism happening out there.

At first, I just sit and stare. I'm not a prude by any stretch of the imagination, but I was born in the freaking 1600s so it is a bit of an adjustment. I'm a tattoo artist, not a fucking nun, but damn—this is definitely outside of my wheelhouse.

As soon as we sit, a waitress in a gold gossamer dress, thin enough she might as well have been naked, sets two martinis down on the table for us. Mine matches my dress, and Striker's matches the exact shade of his crimson tie. I give our waitress a sweet smile, staring at her face and not her assets in an effort to be polite, and pass her a twenty for the swift service. I keep Striker's words in mind and make sure I don't touch her skin. I'm not sure if the bartender rule trickles down to the waitresses or not, and it's not the time to ask. Striker frowns at me for tipping, but as a rule he knows if I don't pay for my drinks, I always tip.

The waitress is thin and pixie-like, her flaxen hair a fine sheet down her back as she gives me a grateful grin on crimson lips and flounces away. Striker and I tilt our heads to see if she's wearing any underwear beneath her thin toga-like dress. She isn't.

I feel very overdressed in a club like this—like I should be naked, or at least wearing a teddy or something. It's ridiculous. Other than Striker, who is killing it in a well-tailored navy suit, I'm wearing the most non-see-through fabric in this joint. I raise an eyebrow at Strike, giving him my best "what the fuck" face.

"When you said orgy, you weren't lying."

"You act like I exaggerate on a regular basis."

"You do, and you know it."

"Okay, but I didn't this time, so it should lower my average."

"So lowered."

Striker nods, grinning as he sips his martini, and the pair of us settle in to gawk at the sheer debauchery going on within our field of vision. The dance floor is like a conga line—if that particular conga line just so happened to involve penises. I tilt my head this way and that. There are big ones, curved ones, regular-sized ones. So many. And I'm pretty sure there are a couple of acrobats getting it on in the ribbons. Seriously, this is better than porn.

"Is this a sex club? Did you honestly bring me to a witch sex dungeon, Strike?"

"Of course not! This is a regular club. The sex clubs are way worse."

How in the high holy fuck could a club be any more depraved than what I'm seeing blows my mind.

We're in the booth for maybe ten minutes when Strike gets a visit from a statuesque blonde woman begging to dance with him. By begging, I mean instead of talking directly to him, she drapes herself across his lap and plants a hot kiss on his lips. I'll give her credit where it's due because she's rocking the shit out of a pair of black leather pants and a baby pink see-through lace bustier. Plus, her assets are substantial. I don't even have to strain to see her nipples, so I know Striker is practically salivating after her. I don't even swing that way, and I am.

What is in these drinks?

Striker raises his brows at me, and I'd be a shitty friend if I didn't let the man blow off some steam. I shoo him, letting him off babysitting duty for a little while.

Pink Bustier Girl doesn't lead Striker to the dance floor. She diverts at the last second and directs him to a tall man in a dark suit with a faint mobster vibe, but in a hot way. With dark hair pushed back off his forehead, paired with piercing blue eyes, I get the feeling he's someone you'd like to look at, but isn't a man you'd want to cross in a dark alley.

Striker seems to know him, though, and his posture doesn't suggest he's in any trouble, so I let him have his privacy and go back to people-watching. Everyone is having a good time. Usually in a club there is at least someone pissy or a chick crying or someone arguing in a corner, but here there's nothing like that. Is it the drinks, the atmosphere, or the lack of humanity in the room?

I take another sip of my drink and watch some more.

I'm sitting by myself sipping on my third electric blue martini when a man plops himself down in our booth. It's so dark and tucked away here, I can't quite make out his face, but I can see the fullness of his lips and the blinding white of the smile against smooth, dark copper skin. His voice is deep and rough when he asks for a sip of my drink.

"I don't think so." I laugh incredulously. I mean, who in the hell does this guy think he is, sitting in my booth and begging a drink off of me? It doesn't matter how cute he seems. Or how well his pecs and biceps seem to fill out his shirt. Okay, maybe it matters a little, but dammit. This is my drink.

"And why not, pretty lady?" His voice is a purr of a jungle cat, and he is just as lithe as he scoots closer. He smells divine. Like man and a subtle hint of really good cologne. His dark-brown eyes seem black in the low light, but regardless of their shade, I'm pinned to this slick booth like a butterfly on display.

"You can get your own drink." I'm pretty sure I don't mean for my voice to sound so husky, and I definitely don't mean to be as flirty as I am.

"Not without tipping off the bartender I don't belong here," he denies, sliding closer into my bubble of space. I lean into him a little, and I don't know if it's because we're surrounded by a hundred people having sex, or the seriously potent liquor I've consumed, or maybe it's just him, but I am seriously drawn to this mystery man who seems to have fallen into my lap.

Get it together, girl.

"That makes two of us. The waitress brought me mine, just wait for her to come back and we can order you one," I offer trying to get a handle on the situation, taking a sip to fortify myself.

"That will take forever. What do I have to do to convince you to share?" he asks, his lips brushing mine as he speaks, his tongue tasting the bite of alcohol still on them.

And then we're kissing. I'm no shit kissing a complete stranger I probably could not even identify in a police line-up, but at this point, I'm either drunk from whatever juju they put in the martinis, or just on him since I find myself pulling up the skirt of my dress pretty fast so I can straddle him.

The heat of his body against mine, of his lips against mine, scratch an itch I didn't know I had. His fingers dip into the gathered bust of my dress, and he nearly makes it to one of my nipples when a huge bang and screams ring out. The pair of us freeze, the heat of his hands at my hips before I'm yanked off the man's lap. Striker's warm touch circles my bicep as the fog lifts from my mind, and I yank my skirt down.

The man I was straddling let loose a wicked-sounding growl, but Striker is already pulling me away from him and toward a side door.

"We've got to go. Fast. It's a raid. We do not want to be within five miles of this place," he shouts, and hauls me away from the throng of people streaming away from the dance floor. People are screaming, and men are shouting. I trip, nearly falling on my face, but Striker hauls me up before I can biff it.

I don't know what's going on, but I know enough to know it's bad. Is this club not allowed? And who in the hell is raiding a place like this? It isn't like we have witch police out to stomp out fun. Or maybe we do, and I just don't know about them due to the fact I got kicked out of my coven ages ago.

The red of magic light flashes past us, exploding

against the wall—sealing a side door shut and cutting off our immediate escape route. Striker lets loose a growl that vibrates down his arm, and I know we're in the shit now. We break left, skirting around naked revelers as they flee to the exits. I nearly fall again, and this time, Striker's ready for it, seeing as he hauls me over his shoulder in a fireman hold, knocking the breath right out of me. He moves much faster without me slowing him down.

Before I know it, I'm plopped onto the passenger seat of Striker's Tesla and he zips off into the night, leaving that weird little club and a ton of questions in the dust.

But I won't forget what I saw there or the kiss that woke me up.

CHAPTER THREE

MAX - ONE YEAR LATER

Unlocking my shop and setting up is one of the best parts of my day. It took a long time to get back to a place where I didn't freak out when I woke up, didn't panic every time I tried to fall asleep.

Six months ago, I died helping my friends. It wasn't the first time it's happened, but it was the first time in a long time that I wasn't sure if I'd come back. Another witch drained my energy trying to break one of my wards—a ward which was keeping my friends safe. Stupidly, I'd tied it to my life force, so when my heart stopped beating, the ward broke.

Dying that time was the worst one of them all. It was worse than the first time by miles.

I check my calendar, making sure I have designs drawn up for my girl, Alice, who plans on getting a skull made entirely of flowers incorporated into her sleeve. I pull the design and get my area set up.

When she comes in for her appointment, Alice tells me all about her boyfriend who she thinks is cheating on her. I wish I could help, but the last time I cast a truth-telling spell it backfired big time, so I'm hesitant to stick my neck out on this one. Instead, I act the way any normal person would and nod in the appropriate places. When her art is finished, I spray a paper towel with green soap and wipe away the excess ink, revealing the vibrant colors of the flowers.

This. This is why I do what I do. A tattoo artist is almost like a priest or a therapist—without the stuffy school or shitty rules. I can tell Alice already feels better after getting new art. I put that smile on her face. After settling up, I welcome a new customer, and on and on it goes as the shop fills with my other artists.

When the evening shift starts, I check my book again. Striker has a late appointment, and my last appointment of the day isn't one I remember making.

Odd.

I SIT ON MY STOOL, THE BUZZ OF THE TATTOO machine in my hand. The guy in my chair is the worst kind of asshole, and I'm tempted to fuck up his ink on principle.

I won't, but I want to.

The design—made by yours truly—is a nautical theme reminiscent of old Sailor Jerry tattoos but with a solid twist toward realism. I'm also tempted to use my special ink for the waves I'm still working on—the ink I use when I'm weaving a spell into someone's skin. The kind of spell that keeps dicks in pants, fists away from women, and makes rude remarks taste like dirt in their mouths.

I have never been very good at following rules—even my own. Hell, especially my own.

"So, pet, what do you say?" The guy leers at me, his eyes laser-locked on my ample cleavage. His name slips my mind. Mark? Mike? Matthew? I swear I saw it on his paperwork earlier, but was too skeeved out by the air he had around him to properly check. Despite the attractive mask and British accent, I am not sold.

He totally misses it when I roll my eyes and wash more gray into the body of his tattoo. At first glance, he seems good-looking. Dark, expertly coiffed hair, ice-blue eyes, chiseled features, decent set of muscles, dressed in cool-guy chic of a well-worn band T-shirt and a pair of jeans. If you didn't hear him speak in that misogynistically conde-scending tone, or maybe if his facial expressions didn't completely give him away as the twat waffle he really was.

But I know his kind—know exactly what they're capable of. I'd been killed by his kind more times than I could count.

Normally, I would shrug him off. Assholes are everywhere, and I get my fair share of them by being a female tattoo artist with a D-cup and a penchant for low-cut tops and tight pants. I can't kill all of them, right?

But this particular one has a very pregnant girlfriend waiting for him on my shop's comfy couch. I can see said couch through the opening in the Japanese screens that separate my workspace from the next one and give privacy to my clients.

It sits directly adjacent to the mirror-fronted counter, and sitting at the counter waiting for his next customer's appointment is Striker. He's solicitously keeping her company, offering her water, and chatting with the seemingly sweet—if a little clueless—young woman. All the while his tawny eyes look her over.

He meets my gaze and gives me "the look."

I hate "the look." That freaking look has gotten me into more trouble over the last century than my normal shenanigans combined over the previous two. Fuck that damn look. But if he's giving it to me, I know for a fact, I can't deny him.

This best friend shit is for the birds.

I'm still pissed about the witch club he took me to—

and incidentally the last time he gave me "the look." It reminds me of another man's lips and tongue and teeth—reminds me of the scant passing minutes we spent clinging, writhing together at a little-known underground witch club and how I wished I remembered his face better. It had been months—almost a year—since I saw him last. I hated that the club we were in was damn near pitch black. I hated that the strobe lights and fog effect obscured his face. I hated that I was too drunk or too stupid to never get his name. I hated how I only remembered the way the scant light caressed his dark skin and the way his lips stretched into the best smile.

I hated that I couldn't remember more.

Disgruntled, I flick my attention back to my best friend —a best friend that is presently looking more and more concerned with each second that passes as he scans the girlfriend.

Striker is an empath—a breed of witch that nearly died out in the fifteenth century. Striker's family was murdered by a rival coven of witches who didn't want the empaths spying on them. It didn't matter to them that empaths typically try to shut out emotions so they don't go crazy, and they for damn sure don't try to manipulate them unless absolutely necessary. Given that emotion magic is the only kind they can do, empaths are usually considered to be the equivalent of long-living humans. I know different, but I'm one of the few.

Striker wouldn't be this friendly or attentive if the woman didn't need it—pregnant or not. He only gives what people need and must sense the same thing I do. She's in a bad situation with this guy or with the baby or with her family. The possibilities are endless for what could be wrong, but I know for certain the man in my chair is the root problem.

The same man who is currently trying to get a better look down my shirt, and if he moves one more millimeter, I might forget my tenuous relationship with the coven leaders of this stupid country and snap his insipid little neck.

"Take a nap," I tell the asshole in my chair as I snap my fingers, and his eyes instantly flutter closed, his head flopping to the plastic-covered head rest with a decidedly satisfying thump.

Ahh. Much better.

I leave him to his snooze and rise from my stool on my favorite pair of electric-blue patent leather peep-toes. The heel on them is bigger than the average man's dick and pairs nicely with my cuffed black petal pushers, magenta tank top, and my signature blue hair.

"Okay, we don't have a lot of time before he wakes up, so what's going on? He beating you? Doesn't want the baby? I know for certain he's a dirty, lying cheater since he just proposed a long night of me giving him 'what he needs' which he described in explicit detail. So, what else is it?"

"Wh-what? What's going on?" she stutters, unable to wrap her head around my questions.

Maybe it's the fact I surpassed her by three hundred years several decades ago or maybe I'm just jaded, but she seems so young to me. If I were to guess her age, I'd peg her at twenty at a push, but more than likely she's closer to eighteen. Her hair is a shiny sable color, her skin has the rosy glow of an overheated pregnant woman, and her eyes are a pale blue, offsetting her summer tan perfectly. If her eyes weren't wide with panic, and the general deportment lying in wait behind her long-gone smile wasn't leaning toward bald despondency, no one would know she wasn't happy as a clam.

Striker breaks in with his usual calm demeanor and soothing voice, stepping around the mirrored counter to sit next to her. This catches me by surprise. He isn't known for getting too close to a person in pain—it just makes his worse.

"We know you are in trouble. We know you are severely depressed and in pain. We are willing to help get you to safety. Let us know how we can help you," he says in the 'voice.' This one is the one he uses when he wants people to calm the fuck down. This one is laced with power and only works on humans. I swear to Christ if he weren't one of the best tattoo artists in the country, I would tell him to be a hostage negotiator. Better people have spilled their secrets to Striker without even knowing it.

"Ye-yesterday he found the money I'd been hiding to run away with the baby. Before I got pregnant, he beat me all the time, but now that he knows he's having a son, he wants me to give birth and then take him from me. I heard him talking on the phone to someone. He's going to kill me as soon as I give birth. He wants to sell my baby. I don't—I don't know what to do. I've tried going to the cops, but..." She trails off for a moment. "I know he'll find me. I know he will." Her voice is a trembling whisper as her shoulders heave, and she begins to cry.

Striker must not have given her enough juice, because typically when someone gets hypnotized, their voice is all monotone and flat. And there are for damn certain no tears.

"What's your name, Sugar?" I bend down into a closed-knee squat by her quaking knees.

"Me-Melody. Melody Danvers," she stutters as she takes the pristinely white handkerchief Striker offers from his back pocket. Mopping up her face, her eyes float back down to rest on her knees. I know that look well enough.

It's the look of the beaten, of the shamed. I wore that look plenty when I wasn't much younger than her, and I wore it for much longer than I cared to.

I'm getting this girl out of this if it's the last damn thing I do.

"All right, Melody. Striker and I are going to take care of you. Don't you worry. Do you have family? Friends you can go to?" I'm hoping for a little bit to go on. I sure as shit didn't have a family I could fall back on. If she does, then she should count herself lucky.

"Yeah. My family is back east in a smallish town in Indiana. Even Micah doesn't know where. He still thinks I'm from Kansas, the idiot." Melody swipes at her nose with Striker's hanky and smears her mascara. "Shows how dumb I am, right? My good-for-nothing boyfriend doesn't even know where I'm from." Her eyes begin to fill with tears as she stares off in the distance. She shakes her head and sets her jaw. The girl has grit, I'll give her that.

"That's good. It means he won't know where to look. Striker and I are going to have a little logistical discussion and then we're on top of it. You want something to eat? Drink?"

"No, no, I'm good," Melody responds gratefully, her voice meek.

"All right, Sugar. We'll be back in two shakes." I grab Striker by his elbow, leading him to the office we share.

"Tell me you have a plan, Strike," I whisper furiously as I cross my arms underneath my rather generous chest.

His eyes flick down for a split second before a slow grin spreads across his lips. "I didn't, but I do now."

This does not bode well for me at all.

CHAPTER FOUR

MAX

"No. Never gonna happen," I half-shout and then shush myself before I lose my damn mind. "There is no fucking way I am seducing that shitbag. I put him to sleep. Let's just throw his ass in a dumpster in a random alley and give her a really good head start. It doesn't have to be too complicated."

Crossing my arms, I give Striker the death glare—the one that he's seen maybe three times in the last hundred years. The one that says there is no freaking way I am getting any closer to this dude, especially now that I know what he's capable of. Who in the hell hurts a pregnant woman? Honestly? What the hell is wrong with people these days?

"Fine." He throws his hands up in surrender. "We'll go with your plan. I'll go in the safe and grab her some traveling money, but you're going to owe me. My plan would have played on his feelings and made sure he didn't follow for a while, but you're the boss."

Ick. Just ick.

"You're damn right I'm the boss." I stomp to the door while he spins the dial on the safe. I'd snap my fingers to open it, but it's a special anti-magic safe, spelled with enough enchantments to zap the fingers off a deity if they tried to open it without the combo.

I may be self-taught, but I'm a prodigy. *Thank you very much.*

Crossing the room, I peek at Micah, making sure he's still asleep and gently pull Melody to her feet.

"All right, darling girl, we're going to get you out of here. Okay?" I confirm before tucking her under my arm and snagging my purse. We head to the back entrance, ready to slip into my car in the back parking lot, when everything seems to happen at once.

A red-hot hand seals over my wrist and yanks me back, just as Striker busts from the office at my blood-curdling scream.

But I can't look at Striker. I can't process anything except Micah's distorted face and glowing red eyes.

I don't know what he is, but Micah is definitely not human.

Houston, we have a problem.

I've been around for quite a while—not nearly as long as some—and I am well aware of my ignorance at the majority of Ethereal dealings. Almost everything I know is self-taught, so I could fill a freaking library with the shit I don't know. But the current and most important thing I don't know is why in the holy fuck this man's touch burns, and how in the hell did I not realize he wasn't human?

Micah's grip tightens on my wrist, pushing the agony deeper in my tissues—into the bones of my wrist and up my arm—into the very heart of me. I feel the burning everywhere, so much I can barely speak, I can barely think. All I think is *pain, pain, pain,* and then my mind is pulled, sucking into the deep void of my memories. I'm trapped in the one I try the hardest to block out —the memory of the last time I died.

My head aches and my body burns. I've finally done it this time. I don't know if I'll wake up when this is all over. I don't know if this is my last thing. I wish I was smarter. I wish I knew a better way to keep everyone safe.

I wish I learned more before I died the first time.

Something is draining me, and if I had a guess, it's someone stronger than I am, breaking the ward I so stupidly tied to my life force. Like an idiot, I thought no one could break it.

"Umm, guys?" My voice is thready as I sway on my feet. This is happening faster than I thought it could. Before I can go down, Ian is there to hold me up.

"Som-someone is trying to break the ward. Someone is trying to get in the house." I warn my friends. Aurelia has to get out, she has to protect her children.

Everyone braces, but my vision has narrowed down to just my best friend and her daughter in her arms.

They need magic, but I can't help them anymore. I don't have anything left of me and I tell them so.

"You didn't. Please tell me you didn't," Ian begs as he shakes. His face is ravaged, a mask of disbelief and pain so acute he can barely breathe, and I don't know why. I don't know why he cares. This is the same man who hated me on site, who bickers with me at every opportunity. Who insists on tossing insults my way any chance he gets.

But he's so sad right now.

"I can't… do that. Had to make it stronger. Couldn't… leave you unprotected. Had to do my part," I gasp as I fade, the tunnel of vision growing smaller and smaller.

"What did you do?" Aurelia begs.

"I reinforced the ward. Tied it to my power. When she breaks it… Well, you're going to be a man down." I'm trying to make it a little funny, but my friends don't know. They don't know how many times I've died. They don't know what I would give up just to make sure they were safe.

Even if this might be the last time. I've never died like this. I don't know if I'll come back. This is worse than the first time. I didn't have anything to live for back then.

"I had to keep your babies safe, didn't I? It's better me than them. I've lived longer. Sybil's right, you know. Magic. Use it. Get creative, and get those babies out of here. She's coming. Take them, and be safe," I warn, and it's the last thing I say.

I suck in one last breath, and then I can't pull in another. My body wilts, the last of my power leeching from me as my vision dims.

Everything is blackness.

Nothing but an empty void I cannot escape.

THE SCREAM COMING OUT OF MY MOUTH SEEMS to snap me out of the memory of my worst fear. Dying doesn't scare me. Staying dead does. And this man—this thing—is pulling it from me against my will. I know he is, because it's carved into every line of his face—the joy he's taking by making me scream. It's enough to wake me up, enough to make me block the pain for a moment and gasp a spell which could slow him down.

"*Mille vulnere*," I mutter as I snap the finger of my left hand. *One thousand cuts.* I'm not optimistic it will do much more than give him a paper cut, but I have to try.

At the snap, Micah hisses, his grip loosening a fraction

as cuts open up on his face. The open wounds pour blood as black as night—another notch in the "What the fuck" column—so I repeat myself once more, until his grip is loose enough for me to snatch my arm back.

But even though I've injured him, I'm not the only one in his grasp. Striker has Melody behind him protecting her with his body, but he's frozen, held up by his neck with an invisible hand, his toes barely touching the floor. My cuts on Micah are doing exactly jack and squat.

Getting us out of here is my top priority, but I don't have enough juice to do much about it. I could transport us all at full strength, but right now, I feel about as powerful as a wet noodle. My brain feels scrambled, everything is distorted and jumbled.

I open my lips to mumble the spell again, my brain frozen, but before I can utter another word, I'm thrown back—flying across the room until my back slams against the wall, the tips of my toes dangling above the floor—held by an invisible hand at my throat.

Micah is smiling now, the red of his eyes glowing bright with a magic I've never seen before. I don't have the first clue what he could be, and, honestly, I'm not sure I want to know. He gave me the creeps before, and now all I feel is fear.

The incorporeal hand at my throat squeezes, but I

manage to choke out the only spell I can think of to save my ass from dying. *"Exilium." Banishment.*

Micah is shoved back, the hand at my throat falling away as I suck in a staggered breath. *"Exilium,"* I croak, and Striker collapses at my back, coughing.

Micah's shoved back again, and the taint he leaves on the air lightens. I feel the magic rising in me, bubbling up like a volcano about to erupt as I scream, *"Exilium!"* one last time. The green casting light of the spell explodes from my hands. Mirrors and glass shatter, the plaster of the walls crack, light fixtures hum before exploding spraying shards of glass and sparks all over us. And I take a small amount of satisfaction at Micah's face as he's thrown through the plate-glass window of my shop and into the street.

I feel the burning tickle of blood seeping from my nose as the world tilts. *Too much. That was too much magic,* I think as I wilt to the floor. My only solace is the blaring horn and sickening crunch of what I hope is Micah being run over by a truck sounding in my ears before the world tilts one last time and my body gives out.

Everything is blackness, and I'm starting to hate the dark.

I WAKE UP TO A BLISTERING HEADACHE, DRAPED

on a very familiar couch. It's mine, a comfy slate-gray leather that's buttery soft. I'm uncomfortable, my burned wrist trapped underneath me, but my shoes are off, at least, which is a considerate bonus.

I hear the rumble of Striker's voice somewhere deep in the recesses of my West Highlands ranch, and the faint yet hysterical tones of Melody asking him what the hell is going on. I get it. Everything she has ever known has just been turned on its ear. But I'll leave Striker to explain it to her. Hell, he might even be able to calm her down, but even his abilities have limits.

I abandon the couch and my shoes, searching for my best friend and our new charge. What I find is Striker holding Melody in a gentle embrace, his lips brushing her forehead. It's sweet and heart-wrenching, and I hate that this happened to her, but I'm glad she made it into our shop today.

I abandon my guests and walk right out the front door. I don't know what Micah was, and I don't want to know. What I do know is this house has to be re-warded and pronto. I pick my way through the cool grass, stopping at the stone retaining wall surrounding my property and start the chants.

I don't ward the same way other witches do. Which makes sense since I'm not a regular witch. We are supposed to be taught spells and castings before we can even read—the natural magic flowing through us like water. But Mama never taught me the right way to do anything. I wasn't instructed on how to do even basic things that every witch knows how to do. Mama was more concerned with hiding my innate abilities and keeping her seat at the table.

She said I was too powerful—my body held too much. She couldn't trust me, she'd said. Told me if I didn't stop flaring my power, she'd bind me—stealing my abilities away and leaving me as defenseless as a human.

I'm actually surprised she never bound me, never took my power away to keep her precious status. I suppose coming back from the dead only to be cast out of my coven was punishment enough. To this day, I still don't know if I was too powerful for her or if my abilities just embarrassed her.

I suppose I'll never know.

I curl my toes into the wet grass, muttering the protection spells which should keep us safe. Whatever Micah was, this should keep him out. My only hope is, he was either dead or too out of it to follow us. But knowing what I do about the Ethereal, I don't trust Micah is anything close to dead.

I walk the perimeter of my property three times, marking the dirt every ten feet or so with a sigil for protection. I'm on my fourth pass out of ten when Striker finds me.

"Overkill much?"

"You and I both know this isn't overkill. This is barely the tip of the damn iceberg." Something in my gut tells me we are in for a world of hurt.

CHAPTER FIVE

MAX

Taking another look at the quiet residential street my house sits on, I wonder if any of them know what I am. Wonder if any of them are even a little like me. Alone. Outcast. Plodding along day by day, still stinging from a hurt that refuses to go away. I sometimes wonder what my neighbors must think of me—the blue-haired tattooed woman pacing a circle around her yard, burned and bloody.

It's a miracle no one calls the cops.

But then I remember the illusion charm I put on the four points of the retaining wall when I moved in four years ago. They don't see me broken and bloody. They only see me walking around my yard. They also get the impression I don't want visitors, so they don't talk to me.

Hiding is a lonely life indeed.

"I hate to break it to you, but you're going to have to come inside at some point," Striker insists at my back as I complete my tenth pass of warding my house and property. Yeah, I'm acting like a nut job, but Striker didn't see what Micah put in my head.

He didn't relive the worst moment of his life at the whim of a sick fucking asshole. His mind wasn't invaded and defiled. I shudder and wipe my nose. It comes away red, but I don't have the luxury of stopping right now. I need to make an obfuscation charm for each of us and get Melody the hell out of here.

"You and I both know you're better with people than I am. You explain it to her. Better yet, explain it to me. I haven't a single freaking clue about what that was." I'm half-hysterical as I throw up my hands and head to my greenhouse. The arid Colorado weather isn't conducive to growing some of the more sensitive plants I need for spells, so I had it built when I had the kitchen redone. For about a month, my wards and my sanity were total shit.

The matte-black steel frame bisects thick-paned glass walls all butting up against an eight-foot stone wall that was already on the property when I bought it. I had the foundation and frame specialty made by an expert welder who had a general contracting business. He made the entire thing by hand in under three weeks, constructing everything else with a team. The back wall was a pain in the ass to work around, but yards in this part of town aren't exactly huge, so I had to make do with what I had.

Concrete counters hold my heaviest beds, and the cedar shelves carry the smaller pots of herbs. I managed to get running water and a sink in here, but only because Striker charmed a guy with his voice voodoo.

Striker leans against the sink—the product of his hand-iwork and crosses his arms. I recognize this as his serious stance, but I'm not prepared for what comes out of his mouth.

"If I had to venture a guess, I'd go with an incubus. The red eyes are a dead giveaway. He's got some juice, too, if he could hide enough that neither of us realized he was an Ethereal when he walked in."

My brain buzzes for a second before the betrayal sets in. Striker knew what Micah was all along. I've known Striker Voss for more than a century, and never—not once —did I ever hear him talk about an incubus to me. Honestly, we don't talk much at all about Ethereal business.

"Incubus? A—there's such a thing as an incubus? And, B—when the fucking fuck were you going to tell me? For shit's sake, Striker!" My voice comes out as a brittle shout as I viciously snatch sprigs of rosemary and shove them into one of my larger mortars and start grinding.

I can't even look at him right now.

"Well, excuse the shit out of me. It is not my fault your mother taught you exactly dick about being a witch or being a member of the Ethereal altogether. And it isn't like I purposefully hid it from you. Incubi are rare. It isn't like they're on every street corner and I failed to point one out. I haven't seen one in longer than I can remember. Jesus. Calm down."

Oh, no, he did *not* just tell me to calm down.

"Calm down. Calm down? Were you just shown your worst memory? Did you have to relive it? Did you have to relive dying? No? Then shut the fuck up with your calm down," I snarl, the pot of the rosemary plant cracking under the weight of my power filling the air. If I don't stop, I'll bust the windows of the whole greenhouse.

The horror on Striker's face is what does it. He's the only one who has been here for me since it happened. I shut every single person out of my life but him. He's felt it, the fear that claws at me. Fear I hadn't felt since the first time I died.

"Jesus, babe. I-I'm sorry. I didn't know that's what you saw. I just thought he was burning you."

This takes the wind out of my sails. Of course, he couldn't know what I saw.

"Well, he was doing that, too. Speaking of, I need to make a poultice to fix this shit, or it will get infected."

"Which you have in the house. Along with your

candles. You can do just as many spells in your kitchen as you can out here. Quit stalling. I know why you won't come inside, but you're just going to have to get over it."

Striker is reading me—which I hate—but he isn't wrong. I don't want to go inside because I know I'm going to have to face Melody. She's going to be looking at us to tell her what to do, and I have no freaking clue.

"I don't know what to tell her. We said we'd take care of her, but this is way bigger than just an abusive human. That I can fix with a spell and an amulet. This shit I cannot fix, man."

Striker throws an arm over my shoulders and steers me out of my greenhouse, across the courtyard, and toward my kitchen door. Despite the difficulty with the climate, I still have several pots of flowers on the cobblestone patio which serve precisely zero magical purpose. I just love pretty flowers, and witches by nature are typically kickass at gardening.

"Just because you can't fix it, does not mean you get to bitch out when you said you'd help. I know I got you into this mess, babe, but you're just going to have to suck it up for a minute and get your shit together, got it?" Striker lands the truth bomb I did not want to hear.

I grumble something unintelligible and stomp through the doorway, bypassing Melody sitting at my breakfast table and heading straight for the liquor cabinet. I'm going to need a big glass of bourbon to get through this shit. I pull the bottle down and slosh three fingers into a whiskey glass, downing it in two swallows. I refill the glass and take a seat at the table across from Melody and reluctantly meet her eyes.

"He isn't dead, is he?" she asks, starting off with the hard shit. She looks so young, yet the fear and pain in her eyes tell me she's lived through enough hell to last a lifetime. Striker must feel the waves of fear coming off of her, too, because he's right behind her, rubbing her back.

"Doubtful, darling. Very doubtful."

"That was…" She pauses to try to wrap her head around it, I assume. "He isn't human. I thought I was going crazy, but I'm not, am I? He has red eyes. I didn't imagine that." She sounds almost relieved, and I wonder how much of the stress Striker felt coming off of her was her worry that she was mentally ill.

"No, sweetheart, he isn't human. In case you were wondering, we aren't, either." I don't know if she realizes this, and honestly, I don't want to have this conversation later.

She rolls her eyes in a "no shit" way, which only people under the age of twenty can truly master but seems to soften it with a little half-smile.

"I caught that part. But you're nice, right? I mean, you aren't going to hurt me. You aren't like Micah."

She seems so young to endure what she has—what she's still—facing. Too young to have the weight of a child coming into the world, too young to have a man beat her. Not that there is any age where that would be a good time, but for it to happen to her so young...

"No." I repress a shudder. "We aren't like him. I've locked down the wards, so we should be good for the night. How about I get you some food and set up in my guestroom for tonight, and in the morning, we can figure out how to get you out of here? How does that sound?"

Melody's smile is grateful as she nods, and I hope by the time she actually needs me, I can come through for her.

I TOSS AND TURN THROUGHOUT THE NIGHT, finally giving up on sleep at about two in the morning. I should be exhausted. I should be passed the fuck out in my massive bed, but the curling pit of dread in my belly isn't having it. Typically, I sleep in the nude, but the fact I have guests in my house nips it in the bud. The stretchy silk camisole and matching sleep shorts should be comfortable, but unfortunately, they're binding. Maybe that's it. My tits are pissed they can't roam free and are punishing me with no sleep. I'd like this better than the alternative.

Because the alternative is the nagging worry my wards aren't strong enough. That the amulet I put on Melody isn't strong enough. That I need a lot more help than I'm willing to ask for. I love my friends. I love the whole Constantine Clan. But the fact of the matter is, I died and came back in front of them, and I just can't face them if they think what my mother thought. I couldn't stand it if they didn't give a shit about me anymore because they think I'm something I'm not.

My mother thought I was cursed or a necromancer when I woke from being burned at the stake. She didn't even ask me. She just cast me out without a second glance. As if I was dead to her—as if I meant nothing.

I couldn't bear it if the only real family I have did that, too.

I throw the covers back, grumbling at the misfortune of runaway sleep and abandon my room in search of ice cream. And maybe some more bourbon. The house is quiet, not even the usual settling of the house due to the dry Colorado heat. It's eerie in a way I don't like, and I can't tell if it's my body's way of recognizing danger, or if I just locked my wards down so tight even the summer heat decided to fuck off.

Opening the freezer drawer, I pull the triple fudge gelato out and contemplate just eating directly from the carton. I live alone, and other than Striker, rarely have guests, so it isn't exactly out of my wheelhouse to eat the whole thing by myself. I reluctantly decide on a bowl and spoon since if I were a pregnant lady in a house full of strangers, I wouldn't want someone's germs while I ate fudgy goodness.

The hair on the back of my neck stands on end as the prickle of one of the wards breaking flashes across my skin. *Son of a cock sucking motherfu...*

"Striker! Melody!" I have to get them up. They need to be awake, and we need to get the hell out of here. How am I going to get them out of here? Striker doesn't have the ability to transport himself like I can—the freaking slacker —and this is when I have enough juice.

But I can't do a transport of three people. I sure as shit can't do it after what happened in the shop. I knew I was powerful, but I've never destroyed a room like that. I've never had to exert that kind of power—drain it, sure—but not like that.

Snap. Another ward breaks.

Striker bounds into my living room, wearing a pair of striped pajama bottoms he seems to have conjured from thin air and nothing else, with Melody trailing behind him in what I'm assuming is his T-shirt stretched over her pregnant belly.

I'd be half-tempted to give him shit if it weren't for the third ward break whipping against my skin. Wards are no better than a deadbolt. Anyone can pick anything if given enough time.

The fourth ward breaks. This time, I actually feel the snap of it cutting into my skin as a rivulet of blood drips from an open cut on my cheek.

This isn't picking the ward like a lock—this is bombarding it with enough brute-force magic so it falls like a domino. And even though I tied it to the earth and not myself, I may be in some deep shit.

I wipe away the blood and show Striker.

"Shit," he rumbles, his eyes flashing.

Shit is right.

CHAPTER SIX

MAX

Striker's tawny eyes focus on the red staining my fingertips, and a preternatural growl slips past his lips. Strike isn't mixed with any form of shifter—I don't think—so that growl is pretty impressive. And my focus on it is my coward-ass way of not dealing with the shitty situation right in front of me. I'd rather contemplate the supernatural quality of Striker's pissed-off growl than deal with this.

Because I can't really process all my wards breaking. I can't process the blood on my face. I cannot fucking handle this. It isn't what happened the last time I died, but it is too close for comfort.

I promised Melody I would take care of her—promised I would help her see this through—and here I am losing it at the first freaking turn. I'm ashamed of myself. How in the hell did he find us, anyway? My place was warded out the ass.

Did someone follow us? And how does he have the juice to break through a ward like this? The only time my ward has been broken was by a host of evil souls—hundreds, maybe thousands of souls bound for Hell by a witch determined not to die.

That, I totally get. This? Not so much.

The fifth ward breaks, and this time it nicks the skin of my neck—a thin stream of blood runs right across my windpipe. It isn't deep, but it's enough to hurt.

At my pained gasp, Striker goes into damage-control mode—something which is usually my job—and looks out the windows, assessing the situation while I try to get my shit together.

"There are five pairs of red eyes out there. Your baby daddy have buddies, Melody?" Striker's voice comes out calm, but I know he is pissed beyond all belief.

"Y-yes. He has friends. I didn't know they were like him." She shudders, rubbing the large swell of her belly. None of this can be good for her. Neither will murder right after giving birth, so I need to fucking focus.

"We need to get the hell out of here, Max. Please tell me you have a plan."

Is he high? A plan? I'm lucky I'm not pissing in my pants right now, and he wants me to come up with a plan?

But it's true that out of the two of us I'm usually the one to get us out of a mess. Sort of. Sometimes. Okay, it's usually fifty-fifty.

My expression must convey my thoughts on the matter because he grabs me by the shoulders and gives me a little shake. Not enough to hurt, just enough to snap me out of it. Hell, at this point a solid slap to the face would be welcome. I'd really love to wake up and have this be some shitty little nightmare.

But I know it isn't.

"What about a doorway? You can make one of those, right?" Striker offers the idea like he's trying to calm a feral cat.

I haven't made a doorway in ages. I quit making them after I figured out how to transport myself. But I still know how to make one. I might have the ingredients to do it, but I can't even start the spell until all the wards are down.

"I'd need yarrow and angelica flower from the greenhouse. Salt and chalk, and a bowl of chicken blood. And I couldn't start it until the final ward is broken." My voice is weak and I freaking hate it. Why hadn't I learned how to defend myself? Why wasn't my magic working on this guy? It works on every other type of Ethereal.

"Do you even have the chicken blood?"

Oh, no, he did not just ask a practicing witch if she has

chicken blood. That's like asking a chef if he has fresh garlic.

"Of course I have the fucking chicken blood. It's in the fridge next to the other chicken parts. What do you think this is, amateur hour?" I snap, which is likely the intended response.

"Well, excuse me, Miss Maxima, I had no idea we were working with an actual witch who had her shit together. Welcome back." His tone is snide, and he's only ruffling my feathers by calling me Maxima. I hate that damn name. What in the high holy hell was my mother thinking?

The sixth ward breaks, splitting the skin of my back and causing me to cry out from the pain. This one is deep, and it kicks my ass into gear.

"Striker, grab the yarrow and angelica flower. Melody, grab a stone bowl from the kitchen."

"On it," he says, and I follow Melody in the kitchen and grab the mason jar labeled "CB" since I do *not* need to explain that shit to a visitor, even though I don't really have visitors except for Striker.

In the next moment, Striker stomps back into my kitchen with a terra cotta planter in each hand, and the three of us head down the stairs to the finished basement. Finding the innermost room, my casting room, I snap my fingers and fire blazes from the six tall pillar candles I set strategically around the room. There isn't a light switch here or a real altar. Just a long wooden table with a thick grimoire, vials of salt, chalk, and a hammered metal bowl.

I can't cast this spell with a metal bowl. It jacks with the polarity like a compass going bananas, and then the direction gets really messed up. I pluck the bowl from Melody's hand, and get the set-up started, rather than wait to see what other horrors another ward breaking will do.

I don't have to wait. The seventh and eighth wards break in quick succession in the form of a pair of slashes forming an "X" on my belly, cutting into my camisole pajama top and splitting my skin enough to have me doubled over.

Shit.

If this keeps going, am I even going to be able to do the damn spell?

I suck in a huge breath, grunting through the pain as I struggle to stand. I draw the doorway on the wall with the chicken blood, whimpering as I stretch to make it big enough. Striker's right behind me, drawing a circle of salt around us before handing me the chalk. I shave some chalk dust into the bowl, followed by the rest of the chicken blood, three sprigs of yarrow, and a full bunch of angelica. I have to burn it all together and say the words, but I have two wards left before I can start.

The ninth ward breaking splits the skin of my thigh,

the tenth the length of my left forearm through the already-burnt flesh. It's enough to make my vision dance.

I can't bitch out now, though, so I shake myself and begin.

Mumbling the Latin phrase, I barely get the words out to open the door—the pearlescent light folding this reality to create the portal. Striker goes through first to make sure it's safe. He gives us the high sign, letting us know it's clear, but I know I don't have enough time. The pounding of booted feet are on my stairs. They know where we are, and with no barriers, they can come as fast as they wish.

I look to Melody. She hears it, too—the thunder of them coming. The fear on her face guts me.

I promised I would help her. I swore. And I don't go back on a promise. Ever. I didn't when I was a teenager and it cost me my first life, and I sure as shit won't do it now when it could cost someone else's.

I do the only thing I can think of. Grabbing Melody by the upper arm, I yank her toward the door, which I hope leads to the upstairs apartment of my tattoo shop, and shove her through. She stumbles a bit, but Striker catches her before she can fall. Just like I knew he would.

They'll be good for one another. The way he takes care of her... He'll be a good dad. He'll take care of her, and she'll take care of him. They'll be safe and happy.

I can do this. *I can.*

Then I set out to close the door—keeping them both safe from the men whose only instinct is to kill, to take. Men who will hurt them, kill them, steal Melody's baby as soon as it breathes its first bit of air. Steal her happiness and his. They will take it all away if I let them.

Striker's face right before I close the door behind them tells me all I need to know. This time, when they kill me, I might not come back. He knows this just as much as I do. His expression cuts at me worse than the wards breaking. I'm hurting him, yes, but I'm saving him, too. He might not see it that way, but I can live—or die—with that.

Before the door seals shut, Striker's growl of betrayal reaches my ears. If I don't make it out of here, he'll never forgive me.

If I save them, though, it will be worth it.

CHAPTER SEVEN

MAX

Staggering out of my casting room, I leave a blood trail on the wall holding me vertical.

I am so fucked.

The best I can do is try and get the hell out of here to give Striker and Melody a head start. I don't have enough time to make a doorway, but I might have enough strength to get upstairs.

But I don't make it that far. Micah's red eyes meet me when I turn to the back corner of my basement, and his smile as he wraps his burning hands around my forearms is as evil as it gets. And those awful hands take me back to a day I never wanted to go to again. The day I lost everything.

VIRGINIA 1642

It felt as if ants were crawling across my skin. That urge—that need to get up, to get out, to go away was back. I hated that feeling, but the older I got, the more often it came.

I was born in Spain, but my mother took the voyage to the New World when I was a baby. The Americas were all I knew, and I wondered if this place was any good for people like us. It didn't seem to be. Witches—or more often than not, humans accused of witchcraft—were being killed left and right, and I feared for our safety. If it weren't for the wards which were pressing in on my skin, we would be known to the humans who colonized so close to us.

Despite the climate outside our wards, I could not stay in this bed or this house or this commune one more second, and although my stupidity would be monumental, I still tiptoed on stocking feet across the freshly polished floor to the thick wooden door which led outside.

I'd polished that floor, and every other piece of furniture and bit of silver in our house. I polished shoes, too. I milked the cows, I tended the chickens, I fed the pigs.

What I did not do, was learn anything other than how to tend a house. Valuable information—but not valuable enough.

Mama did not let me practice with the other girls my age. I did not learn the spells I needed to—the spells I should have been taught since I learned to speak.

Which was not to say I did not know some things, but what I knew scared me. I was stronger than the girls my age. I was stronger than all of them put together. I could do things even my own mother could not do. I could do things this entire coven could not—like walk right through a ward as if it wasn't there.

Unlatching the door, I snatched up the boots from their tidy row and stepped out into the night, careful to stick to the shadows wrought by the flickering flames of torches on the walking path. The coven was working something big—every girl my age was attending a ceremony.

Every girl except for me.

It hurt to know I was never going to be included, never going to be the woman my mother wanted me to be, but a large part of myself screamed to get out from under these wards, out from under my mother's thumb.

I was suffocating here under a weight which did not seem to be mine to bear. It didn't seem right that I was the one always on the outskirts of my own family.

Making it to the edge of our land was easy, the only hiccup was walking through the ward hexes without breaking them. As much as I needed to be free, leaving my family unprotected was three steps past stupid and reckless on a scale even I wasn't capable of.

Fifteen wards—one from each of our elders—guarded our land. Not only did humans not cross into our property, any Ethereal would be shocked into unconsciousness and likely trapped in a magical snare very few could escape. Plus, anyone who came within a stone's throw would feel a gut-wrenching urge to leave.

But not me.

Picking my way through the wards, I took my first breath of fresh air. Mist was falling, and I tilted my face to the sky. I wanted to stay there breathing in the cool autumn scent of the forest for a moment before I headed back inside the boundary.

Before I could bring myself to head back in, a man's pained groans caught my ears. I should have gone back inside the wards. I should have, but I didn't. Instead, I followed the sounds of agony to find a man clawing away from the warding snare. It didn't matter that he flashed back and forth between what I assumed was his true form of semi-solid black smoke and his glamour of a human man—the snare still caught him.

His human form was of a well-dressed older man. Wavy light-brown hair fell across his face obscuring his features except for the bright luminescent golden glow of his eyes. The buttons on his waistcoat were polished brass, and his boots were supple leather. He was likely wealthy or at least appeared so, but I knew appearances could be deceiving.

I appeared to be a defenseless fourteen-year-old girl, and I most certainly was not.

Something about the man called to me. I'd never seen an Ethereal like him. Not even in passing. Our coven was secluded—hidden away from everyone and everything else who moved in the shadows of our world. He felt familiar in a way that I could not deny.

I had to help him. Had to.

But the only way to help him was to drop the wards—to put my family in danger. It was wrong. It was the worst idea I could think of.

"S-s-s-s-save m-m-m-me..." The thought hissed through my head, but I knew I hadn't heard a sound. It wasn't my voice, it was his.

"I will," I promised, but I didn't tell my mouth to do so. It was as if my mind had been taken over by someone else. The closer I got to him, the more I needed to do whatever I could to make sure he lived.

Without my mind telling my feet to do so, I pivoted toward the hex marks of our coven's ward, snapping the protection spells one by one, until the snare around the man's foot fell away.

"S-s-s-s-save m-m-m-me..."

Then I found myself whispering words of healing—spells too advanced for my young body to handle. A smarter part of me screamed to stop, but I couldn't halt the Latin falling from my lips or the charged green light flickering from my hands.

I was not in control, and I had a sinking feeling that this man, whoever he was, had taken over my body and my powers to free himself. Blood dripped from my nose, and I crumpled to the wet bracken of the forest floor—my legs too weak to hold me up before I regained control of myself.

The man lay there—his form still, glamoured as a human. He appeared to be sleeping, his eyes closed, and his brow unfurrowed, but a large part of me knew better.

I had to get away from him—whoever he was—before he took control over me again. But I didn't get the chance. The sound of hoof beats hit my ears, and their simple squelching echo was enough to put a pit of fear in my belly.

Horses meant men. Men meant humans. Humans who could have seen me do magic. Humans who all too frequently burned women alive for even the assumption of practicing magic.

I didn't have enough time to put the wards back up. I didn't even have enough time or energy to run.

A pair of footmen grabbed me by my elbows, wrenching me from the forest floor and away from the man who was anything but.

They shouted at me, calling me witch and demon. They spat in my face and tore at my clothes, searching for a devil's mark. It wouldn't have mattered if I didn't have one. The footmen were in the employ of a magistrate who rode in the coach, which happened to be passing by.

They thought I killed the man who was lying so still in the mud and leaves that he appeared dead. They saw the green light coming from my hands—they saw my magic.

Without a chance to speak for myself, they tied me to a tree, took a lantern from the coach, and threw it at my feet—the glass and fuel exploding as it hit the base of the oak.

Flames caught the cotton of my dress first, and sooner than I thought possible, I was left to scream out my dying breaths alone as men watched me burn.

Blackness consumed me for what seemed like eternity. I was alone in the dark and I worried over every wrong I'd done and every mistake I'd made in my short life. I was stuck and freezing, and so, so scared.

Eventually a pinprick of light came in the darkness, and I followed it until I could open my eyes and take a new breath.

The forest looked different. A circle around my naked and freezing form was black as night. As black as the void where I had come from. A folded stack of clothes and a pair of boots sat just outside the ring of charred earth, and I fell on them, wrenching the dress and stockings on as fast as I could.

Once I was dressed, I noticed my mother standing not far off, but she didn't seem happy at all to see I was alive.

In fact, when I took a step toward her, she took a step back.

"Mama..." I trailed off, not knowing what I could say for myself. I didn't know how I could even survive the hell of burning and come back unscathed. I didn't know anything anymore.

"You are not my daughter. You are not a member of this coven. You are banished. You are Rogue. No coven will take you. No coven will accept the abomination you have become."

Every word from her mouth was a blow. I knew I should not have dropped the wards, but I wasn't in control. And abomination? How?

"I don't know what happened. What happened to me?"

"You are not a witch. You are something else, and I will not let you taint us any longer."

"But, Mama. I don't understand. How am I alive? I burned. I died," I whispered through sharp sobs which seemed to cut at my chest. "What happened to me?"

"What happened is, you put us all in danger. You took our home from us. You nearly killed us. You tore away every protection we had and now we have to settle somewhere else."

"But I wasn't in control. There was a man made of smoke. He was trapped in the ward snare. He made me free him. I didn't want to. He took over my mind, Mama."

The color leeched from my mother's face, but she didn't answer me. She didn't do anything but snap her fingers, and in a flash of red light, she left me in that forest alone.

MICAH'S SMILE IS THE FIRST THING I SEE WHEN the vision of my past fades. Red eyes and the smallest glimpse of white fangs peek from the sneering uptick of his mouth. Good to know I'm amusing at least.

"So, I'm not the first demon you've met. Interesting. I'd wondered…"

The man from my past—the one who got me killed, the one who ruined my life—was a demon? There are demons?

It didn't really matter. The vision was long, and his power to see my worst memories had an added benefit he didn't anticipate—they made me angry. An angry witch—at least this angry witch—isn't someone to be trifled with.

Micah still had my forearms in his grip, but every red-blooded girl knows the best way to break a man's hold on her. Kneeing Micah in the balls is as satisfying as one could expect. Good to know that part of his anatomy is equivalent. By the time he can catch his breath, I've transported myself out of my basement.

I land on my hands and knees in a glittering pile of shattered glass. Not my best landing, but I still give Striker a tremulous smile when he makes it to me, sliding through broken glass on now-booted feet.

He doesn't catch me, though. The floor does when I lose my fight against the dark.

CHAPTER EIGHT

MAX

The crick in my neck is what hauls me from the blackness. That and the gentle rocking of a moving car. I pop up from what appears to be the back seat of an SUV and panic for a second, until my eyes land on Striker's blond curls and square jaw.

Calming down, I gauge my surroundings. First off, my wounds are bandaged—white gauze and medical tape cover the majority of my forearms. Aches and pains make themselves known throughout my body, and I'm in a new outfit—a decidedly less bloody one of loose black linen drawstring shorts and a gray T-shirt, with a little pocket over the right breast. Said breasts are encased in a black camisole, and based on the level of squish, it has an attached shelf bra. The clothing is familiar since it's mine, and likely procured from my spare closet in the apartment above the shop.

I could be embarrassed about the fact that I did not dress myself, but if Striker did it, then he's already seen everything. Hell, he's done most of the artwork on places which are only accessible by way of complete nudity. He did the dragon that spans from my left shoulder blade over my ribs and down my abdomen to wrap around my left leg. I was pretty much naked for about a month.

I spy Melody in the passenger seat munching on beef jerky and I figure with the heaviness to her belly, it would be unlikely that she would have helped the unconscious woman into new clothes.

"Oh, good. You're alive. I worried I was going to have to bury your rotting carcass in one of these Fate's forsaken corn fields," Striker quips as he passes back a bottle of water, his eyes never leaving the road. He's right. We are beset on both sides by never-ending cornfields on a straight highway which seems to go on forever.

I take the bottle and chug half of it in a few gulps.

"So happy I didn't inconvenience you too much. Where are we? How did I get here? And holy shit on a stick, darling, your ex is the fucking worst," I address Melody. She gives me a sidelong no-shit stare as she shoves another piece of jerky in her mouth.

"We're somewhere in Iowa on the way to Indiana. I

figured the further we were from Micah the better, considering every time you tangle with that dickhead, you pass out. Speaking of, everything but the burns have healed. I don't know what the hell is up with that nonsense."

"How long have I been out?" The not-healing bit isn't great. I don't know what's going on there.

"About twenty-eight hours." Granted, I don't heal exceptionally fast in comparison to other Ethereals, but at the twenty-eight-hour mark I should be pretty close to good. And if I died, well, I typically don't come back with injuries.

"Was I unconscious or the other thing?" I pitch my voice lower since I don't know how much weird Melody can handle.

"You mean dead?" Melody accuses. "Yeah, we had that scare already, but no. You were just unconscious. Thanks for that, by the way. I so enjoy feeling like shit because people stepped in to help me and got hurt. What the hell?"

Melody may be an infant compared to me, but impending motherhood has turned her into one round-bellied mama bear complete with a glare only a real mom could accomplish.

"Well, excuse me for saving both of your lives and getting out in one semi-charred piece. Reliving being burned alive was super fun," I shoot back, my snark at peak level.

"No one asked you to do that. You could have come with us. You could have closed the door and been on the other side. You could have been safe. Instead, you decided to play cowboy and got yourself hurt. Again. Not. Cool." Striker's low voice hits me like a slap.

My leaving really hurt him. I didn't assume he'd like the fact I put him in charge of Melody, but I honestly didn't think I had enough time to get through and close it behind me. I honestly didn't think I could keep them safe.

I didn't think, and that more than anything is the problem. He has been stewing on this for a while now, and even with Melody here, he can't control the venom in his voice.

"What would you have had me do? I put the both of you first. I made sure you were safe. I could barely stand, so I knew I couldn't walk through anything, let alone the doorway. I did what I thought was best, and I'm not sorry, so we'll just have to agree to disagree. Now, is there a rest stop in our future because I haven't peed in over a day and I'm about due."

AFTER ANOTHER THIRTY MINUTES OF TENSE silence, we finally find a rest stop. I race Melody to the bathroom, and I manage to get there first, pee, and wash my hands before she can waddle her butt to the door with Striker keeping pace so she's not alone. Dammit, they are so cute together, I can't stand it.

We make a stop at the nearby convenience store for snacks and coffee before piling back into the SUV and hitting the road.

It takes us another eight hours, ten rest stops, and three driver changes before we arrive in Melody's hometown on the outskirts of Fort Wayne, Indiana. The sun is setting on the green rolling hills of her family's farm, and I'm hit with a pang of loneliness I didn't know I could have. This farm makes me homesick for a home I've never even had.

The scene is idyllic with a sprawling ranch house, a painted red barn in the background, and clear pond close to the road that reflects the summer sky. It looks like a home—something I wouldn't really know about, nor have I experienced in my long life. The dirt road that leads to a farmhouse is enclosed by a horse gate, which Striker jumps out to open so we can pull through.

An older couple—maybe early fifties—meets us at the mouth of the driveway that curves just to the left of the porch stairs. They fall on Melody like a pair of love-starved wolves, as they hug her and kiss her hair. Her mother puts gentle hands to the large swell of her belly, and a sick part of me can't handle it. It can't possibly handle a show of this much love and support.

It isn't to say that I'm not happy she's safe, I am. I am thrilled beyond fucking measure. Unfortunately, I am also a jealous cow because I cannot stop the bitter pang in my chest that wonders why I've never had this.

My mother hated me from the gate, and my father was nowhere to be found. I've never heard my mother speak of him, and if I had a guess, he was the reason we left Spain in the first place. The only place I've had love at all is in Striker's friendship and the Constantine's family. How sad it must be for me to be jealous of a child's love. I manage to get myself under control before I step out of the SUV, but not before I get a look from Striker that tells me he read every single emotion that has ran through my body.

I don't like being read. I don't like that he knows how weak I've been in the last forty-eight hours. I don't like that I've been weak at all. Maybe it's due to the fact I've been forced to relive the deaths that have marked me so, but I feel as if I've been cursed for a very long time.

Scott and Nadine invite Striker and I into their home without a second thought. Genuine hospitality seeps from their every pore and action. Nadine fusses over my injuries, which we were very vague about when recounting the story to Melody's parents.

The pair of them swear up and down that Striker and I

saved their baby girl from an evil man (*very true*) and refused to hear another word about it. Well, Nadine didn't want to hear another word. Scott took Striker and I aside and wanted to know what Micah looked like, and whether or not he should tell his county sheriff about him.

This was a quandary, because if Micah were human, I'd say hell yes. But since he isn't, Striker and I were going to have to be real smooth with how we protected this family. Finally, it was decided that I would walk the grounds and ward as I went.

"Melody, how about you show me around?" I offer as a cover as I usher her outside, and we make a small circle at the main perimeter of the lawn.

"I need to do this circuit ten times. Can we do that and not wig out your parents?" I ask, muttering in Latin as I stop every ten feet.

"Probably. Honestly, I think we should just tell them. Mama is part Cherokee. My grandma taught us the old ways. She'd take it to heart, and we'd be safer if we knew where to step and where to stay safe."

Melody's offer has merit. I've never been a big fan of keeping people in the dark—especially about their own safety.

"Are you sure?" I hedge, unwilling to make a decision without Striker's assessment. He's better at reading people than I am, obviously.

"I'm pretty sure. Plus, who knows what abilities this kid will have. I'm going to bring a child into this world, and I have no idea what he'll become. I'll have to contend with more than may be rational, and they will, too. At least if I tell them now, I'll have you two as backup in case they want to cart me off to the mental institution," she says with a self-deprecating smirk. She's joking, in a "ha-ha, this could really happen so don't leave me," kind of way.

Just then, Striker sidles up to us and wraps an arm around Melody's shoulders. She sort of melts into his side for a moment, and I can't help but smile. Striker is at least four hundred years her senior, but in that tiny bit of time, his eyes don't take on the weight of the centuries he's spent on this planet. For the first time, he appears almost content.

For the first time in a long time, I wonder if I could live without him. I think if he were this happy, I could.

I so could.

AFTER A NICE HOME-COOKED MEAL, STRIKER AND I sit Nadine and Scott down and explain what really happened to their daughter.

"This is nonsense!" Scott shouts as he shoots up from his seat. He paces his living room, his face red with indignation. Personally, I don't blame him. Who wants to know that the world as they knew it is a lie?

"I assure you, I am not a liar," I murmur, but the volume of my voice doesn't matter. What matters is the green casting light weaving around my fingertips like a sentient yet weightless liquid. Scott's eyes lock on my hands until I snap my fingers and the lights go out. I snap again and they come back on. I flex and relax them, and he watches as the lights in their living room dim and brighten enough to hurt our eyes.

"Th-this is a trick. This has to be a trick," Nadine whispers, her voice tremulous as she watches a lamp she's had for probably twenty years, like it will jump at her at any moment.

"No trick. And I'm not here to hurt you. Or your family. Melody came into our shop afraid and alone. We took her away from the man who hurt her and brought her home. The only reason we are telling you anything is because we want to keep her safe just like you do." This seems to placate him a little, and in the end, Scott and his wife believe us—that their safety is all we want.

But when the time came, I didn't keep anyone safe at all.

CHAPTER NINE

MAX

Munching on a likely cancer-causing bit of snack food, I fiddle with Striker's phone, trying to find some good music. His taste in music is questionable at best, but finding a quality radio station during a road trip is a pain in the ass. Every fifty miles or so, the station craps out and I have to switch it again.

Plus, I have a solid aversion to top-forty music. The stations just outside of Chicago weren't bad, but the farther we get from the sprawling city, the less the good stations tune in.

I'm giving Striker shit for his questionable taste in music, trying to perk him up after we left Melody, but I'm not having much luck. He merely stares at the stretch of highway in front of us and periodically grunts at me.

I offered to make my own way back to Denver before we left so he could stay, but Striker's been with me so long, I don't know if he could handle letting me go out on my own. The last few times I did, he was not pleased with the shape I came back in.

I get it, but I wish he would have stayed with Melody. She made him lighter—made him happy. Even though he barely spent more than two days with her, he'd been less bogged down with the emotions of everyone else, and instead, found his own happiness.

It pisses me off that he chooses me instead of himself, but Strike wouldn't be him if he *didn't* sacrifice himself. A part of me recognizes that same irritating quality in myself.

What a pair we are.

When the phone rings in my hand, I fumble and nearly drop it on the floorboard. Melody's name flashes across the screen and for some reason—even though I haven't answered the phone—I know it's bad. I answer the call, my heart sinking to my feet at her panicked whisper.

"Max! You have to come back. He's here. I do-don't know what to do."

I look at Striker. He can't hear what she's saying, but he can feel my emotions well enough. I mouth "turn around" as I try to affect my most calming voice. Inside, I'm screaming.

"Okay, darling. Here's what I want you to do. Find some salt. Your mother keeps a ton of it in the kitchen, right?"

I pull my mouth from the receiver. "Find a building, whatever. We need cover," I tell Strike, noticing the knuckles of his fingers turning white as he grips the steering wheel hard enough to bend it. I need to make a doorway, and I can only do that against a wall or building. I sure as shit can't do it on the side of a busy highway for everyone to see.

"Y-yes. But he has Mama and Daddy. He-he says he'll hurt them if I don't come out. Max, I'm scared." The pain in her voice is like a lash against my skin.

Micah will most likely kill them either way, and that fact hurts so much. She has to know that. She can't do what he wants—not ever.

"I know, baby girl, but he'll hurt them even if you do what he wants. Find the salt, Melody." I try to stay calm. I don't want her to hear the guilt. I don't want her to know that I'm just as scared as she is.

I hear some rustling around and a cabinet slamming before she comes back.

"Okay, I've got some."

"Good. Make a ring around yourself. Thick as you can. It will offer some protection. Striker and I will be there in two shakes, you got it?"

"Ye-yes. You're coming for me, right? Striker's coming, isn't he?" Her voice breaks on the end, and it whips at me like another lash.

For some reason, I'm so glad Striker can't hear the desperation in her voice. The fear. I'm glad these words won't be what wakes him up at night if we don't make it.

"Striker and I are coming. We will always come for you, okay, darling girl? Always. You hang tight."

I disconnect and grab the oh-shit handle as the SUV fishtails when we take the next exit a bit faster than recommended. Still, Striker manages to not roll us and pulls into a storage facility. One of those places for people who have too many things.

"Please tell me you packed my shit," I pray to myself more than asking Strike if he has. I doubt he would have stopped if I didn't have what I needed.

He's at the liftgate before I am, pulling out a black backpack. I don't need much for this spell, but I do need chalk. It isn't like before when I didn't have enough of my own juice to make a doorway and had to resort to using chicken blood. I have more than enough now.

Digging in the pack, I produce the white chalk and draw a rectangle on the brick of one of the storage units. Murmuring the spell, I feel Striker's urgency radiating off of him.

I just hope we aren't too late.

The portal opens into the Danvers' living room. Coming through the doorway, the first thing I smell is blood. Lots of it. A man in horse-working clothes appears to have been disemboweled where he sat on the couch. He isn't Scott, but might have once been a farmhand of theirs. He's young, maybe Melody's age, sweet-looking even in his final rest.

This is who Melody should have been with. She should have stayed in this idyllic country home. Married the sweet farmhand and had his babies. This blood-soaked scene shouldn't be her life.

Over the stench of the recently dead, I try to focus and send my senses out, but the house is still.

"Search the upstairs. Yell if you need me."

Striker is already halfway up the staircase before I get a grunt of assent. He doesn't give one single shit about anything other than finding Melody, and I can't say I blame him.

Moving to the open Dutch door separating the kitchen and living room, my sandals crunch and scrape the broken crockery and salt littering the floor. I skitter to a stop when I see the salt circle in the middle of the room.

It's empty.

The scattered grains are peppered with drops of fresh blood. Melody should still be in that circle. Nothing could have broken that protection that quick. Two minutes. It took us two minutes to get here. It should have been enough time. We should have made it.

Why didn't we make it?

Looking past the circle, little droplets lead to the kitchen door, and I can't stop myself from following them. I feel it against my skin—there isn't another live person here.

I can't figure it out. Why didn't the wards protect them? Why couldn't my magic save them? What makes this guy so much different that my magic does nothing?

The droplets grow more significant as they lead to the porch and turn to puddles that soak the dirt driveway and parts of the grass. In the middle of one of the pools is what I can only guess is Melody's dad. I don't know for sure since Scott's missing his head. And his vital organs. But the fabric of his T-shirt is the same as this morning when he gave me a tremulous hug before we left.

I could tell I made him slightly uncomfortable, which given the light show last night, was warranted. But he still hugged me. Still thanked me for helping his little girl. And the scent of his shirt caught my nose. It snagged my notice because I found it strange that he could have been working before the sun came up, but his shirt still smelled like pipe tobacco and earth. It's funny what one remem-
bers. I still have that smell in my nose, but I can't get my

brain to figure out why the man I knew for such a small measure of time is dead.

I've seen death many times over in my long life. I've seen torture and malice and every concoction of misery a person could think of. But never to this degree.

Never so much violence at once.

Nadine is close by, her puddle slightly smaller, but her evisceration much, much worse. Nadine died last, and Melody had to watch. If not watch, then she heard her screams. I stifle a sob, pressing my palm to my mouth, so I don't start screaming myself.

A trail of blood and gore leads in the direction of the barn. I don't want to follow the path left for me. I don't want to know what lies in wait for me. I just want this all to be a bad dream I can wake up from. I want Melody to be safe.

I don't think I'm going to get what I want.

I pick my way past the gore and follow the trail to the horse barn, danger pricking at my skin with every step. I don't think I'm going to like what I find in here.

At the wide-open entrance, I feel someone coming at me, but I'm ready. I turn to look, and the red eyes are enough to have me snapping my fingers. I watch as the man's head twists on his neck, effectively breaking it as if it were a dry twig.

A faint memory bubbles up. I remember telling Ian

once that I could snap his neck with a flick of my fingers. I was half-joking at the time, irritated at him for using my full name. I wouldn't have hurt Ian, but the amount of satisfaction I feel at the crunch of bones makes me a little sick.

I shouldn't want to smile. I shouldn't feel good for killing someone—even if it is likely temporary.

But I do.

I'm lamenting over my own morality when a knife slashes across my upper back. I was too busy focusing on my own shit, I didn't pay any fucking attention to the fact that Micah had five friends. Yeah, I "killed" one, but there are potentially four others ready and waiting to kill me.

The agony of the blow takes me to my knees. The pulsing lash of white-hot pain flashes across my brain. The kick to the ribs and the subsequent gut twist of a bone breaking catches me off guard. I have yet to see my attacker, but he's kicking my ass something fierce.

Bile fills my mouth as I try to scramble away, but all too soon, burning hands snatch one of my feet right out from under me. My face smashes against the concrete before I'm airborne—tossed like a rag doll into the door of a horse stall. The boards give way under the force and I land half-in and half-out.

One of my arms isn't working, and my burned leg is probably broken.

I'm fucked. I am so fucked.

Adrenaline courses through me—fight or flight my ass. I need to get my shit together or this bastard is going to kill me. I don't want to know what happens if he succeeds.

I can't die right now. I can't. I can't let this thing kill me.

I spy a black double-barrel shotgun propped against the wall in a little cubby next to the open barn door. I need that gun. Using what little power I have left, I snap my fingers, the gun flying into my hand almost faster than I'm ready for.

I press the latch and open the barrel, thankful the damn thing is loaded. I aim, vaguely aware that this might be my only chance.

Pulling the trigger is harder than it should be. Hell, breathing is harder than it should be. But I never hear the gun go off.

I don't hear anything at all.

CHAPTER TEN

STRIKER

When Melody came into the shop, I never expected to be here in her childhood bedroom trying to glean something—anything—about where she is.

It's as if she's just gone.

Not dead.

Gone.

Max thinks I'm merely an empath—a dying breed of witch that no one really gives a shit about unless they are trying to hide something. And in a sense, she's right. It's true, I can feel every single person's emotions as if they are my own. If I didn't ward my mind like Fort Knox, I'd be batshit insane by now.

But I can do things that I don't have an explanation for. can do things that scare the shit out of me. One of them is the ability to tell where a person is—on this side or the other.

If I have a strong mental connection with that person, it is as if I can follow their emotions no matter where they are.

But not Melody. It didn't matter that my gut was filled with worry. It didn't matter that my heart physically ached in my chest every single second since I left her here.

It doesn't matter, because no matter how hard I have tried, I can't find her.

And it pisses me the fuck off.

I'm still trying to glean something from the objects in her room when the blast of a gun rings out, echoing its death knell across the rolling hills of the farm.

I can't say how I made it down the stairs. Or across the lawn past the dead bodies that barely seemed to register. But standing in the doorway of the barn, the scene before me is crystal clear.

Max is unconscious, hanging half-in and half-out of the debris remnants of a horse stall door with a shotgun loosely held in her arms that don't seem to be working. Across the walkway lies an incubus, still as death, and another incubus screaming and clawing at what appears to be the melting refuse of what used to be his face.

And the smell... Sulfur mixed with ass mixed with horse manure.

If I didn't care about whether Max was still breathing, I would give into the bitter urge I have to put my boot in the melting leftovers of his neck and snap it, but Max means more to me than my revenge.

I have to get her out of here. I need to get her to help, and there is only one person I can ask.

Transportation was a problem at first, but I figured Max wouldn't mind if I hijacked her powers for a little while to get us the hell out of here. Another one of my dazzling and altogether unexplainable abilities. I can't exactly use much magic myself, but if the need is great and I put my mind to it, I can play puppet master for a few seconds to get what I need.

I don't like doing it. It makes me feel sick to use some-one, but desperate times and all that.

Arriving on his doorstep with a broken Max in my arms doesn't exactly seem to be a good plan, but I don't have time to rethink it before the door opens to reveal the man I caught Max making out with almost a year ago on that long-forgotten night before the world turned to shit.

"Hey, Ian. I know you're going to have questions, but a little help?" I kind of jiggle Max at him to maybe unfreeze him somewhat.

I don't know if he can't quite figure out how we

bypassed the doorman, if he is pissed we're here at all, or if he just can't process, but he's solid as a statue while Max just keeps bleeding on me.

"Ian!"

My shout seems to snap him out of it, because before I can track it, Max is out of my arms and into his. He turns, hauling ass into his apartment, and I follow, slamming the door shut behind me. A hipster-looking man I've never met jumps to his feet from a black leather couch that looks like it belongs in a frat house, roughly tossing his beer to the coffee table. By a wing and a prayer, the bottle stays right-side up. And he's in a beanie. Who the fuck wears a beanie in July, for shit's sake?

I have no idea at all why I'm focused on that stupid amber glass or his choice of fashion accessories and not my friend.

The shock, I guess.

I think I'd rather think of just about anything but my friend being hurt, or my woman being captured. Maybe I'm stuck on trivial details because if I don't, I'll plan precisely what I'll do to the men who took Melody when I catch them. I'll end up going off half-cocked and screw myself over for sure. Me, I'm not so worried about, but Melody...

"What happened?" Ian sets her on an empty pool table, yanking a black medical bag from underneath it. This preparedness isn't exactly surprising. Ian Moran is known in certain circles as a top-notch doctor, and he doesn't really care which side of the law someone is on as long as they pay.

I doubt I'll have to cough up the dough for Max, but I will if he needs me to.

"I'm not exactly sure. We got separated. Short answer? I have no fucking idea. Long answer? Incubi."

An aghast whistle sounds from the man I've never met, and I nod. A single incubus is a pain in the ass. More than one is a major fucking catastrophe of epic proportions. I was vague as shit when Max asked about them, and not explaining it to her may make me a dick, but I never expected there to be more than one.

Let alone five.

Ian assesses Max, checking her airway before taking a pair of shears to her shirt and bra. What he sees doesn't make him happy at all.

"Aidan, get my surgical equipment. One of her lungs is punctured," Ian barks before hauling ass to the kitchen sink to wash his hands.

He doesn't care that Max has bled all over his once-crisp white shirt. He does not give that first fuck. His manner is a cold-blooded unemotional bag of focus I can appreciate in a medical professional. Aidan grabs a plastic box with a pull-away vellum lid. Inside is a pair of surgical gloves, plastic tubing, gauze, and a scalpel.

Ian dons the gloves before pressing two fingers against Max's left side feeling for her ribs. Then he takes the scalpel and pushes it into her skin.

"Make yourself useful, huh? Grab a bucket," he commands, and I have no doubt he's talking to me. I do what he says, searching his obviously bachelor kitchen for something close to bucket-ish. I find it in one of those plastic margarita buckets one gets in Panama City Beach during spring break.

"Get the lead out!" he calls.

At that moment, I choose not to judge Ian for his obviously sophomoric youth and get the lead out. I offer Aidan the bucket. Ian is already inserting the clamped tube into Max's chest as Aidan holds the bucket at the edge of the table and puts the other end of the tube into it. When Ian unclamps it, a rush of blood runs through the plastic, burgundy lifeblood staining it red.

"Get over here," Ian commands and I hop to. He passes me a face mask with a bag attached. Luckily, I've seen enough re-runs of every single medical drama known to mankind, so I know exactly what I'm supposed to do. Two squeezes of the bag are all it takes for Max to abandon those shallow, panting breaths for slower, deeper ones.

Ian watches her for a few minutes before taking a suture kit to the tube in her chest, and I've never been happier that I don't actually have to look at something that gross.

"Okay, now that Max is breathing again, I'm gonna need you to tell me what the fuck happened to her. Because if you're at fault, I'll find a way to kill your ass, I don't care if I have to make one up." Ian seethes as he ties a knot in the sutures and moves down Max's body to check for more wounds.

A part of me wants to punch him in the face, but I'm finding it difficult to fault the guy. I can sense the love he has for Max—she's it for him. It's likely a wraith bonding trait that he just can't shake. Or maybe it's more. I hope it's more. At least for Max's sake.

"A couple came into our tattoo shop a few days ago. The woman pregnant, the guy a total fuckwad. I could tell the woman—Melody—was in trouble. Max put the guy to sleep, and Melody told us she'd overheard him telling his friends he was going to kill her after she had the baby. Max and I thought we'd just get her out of town, right? But then the guy—Micah—woke up, and he grabbed Max. We got out of there, but he tracked us back to Max's house. We made it out and carted Melody home to Indiana. But, uh... He found her, anyway. Killed her family."

I have to stop there for a moment to clear my throat. I shouldn't be here explaining everything to Ian. I should be trying to locate Melody. I should be using every contact I know to get her back. What if he hurts her? What if she has the baby...

"I was looking for something of hers so Max could locate her. Max was in the barn. Two waylaid her. She took one out, but the other did some serious damage until she got him in the face with a shotgun blast of rock salt."

Aidan whistles again. "Which brings you here."

"Which brings us here."

"What I want to know is why you didn't protect Max. Demons can't touch you—not physically at least. Why didn't you keep an eye on her?" Ian seethes, his eyes flicking back and forth between black and dark brown.

Honestly, I'm stumped. I have no idea what's going on, and I tell Ian as much.

"What the fuck are you talking about?"

"The Armistice, stupid. Demons cannot touch angels and vice versa. Doing so would bring a war no one wants to be in the middle of. You could have protected her if you just stuck with her. They would have left her alone. Sure, she's half-demon, but with an angel in the mix, they wouldn't have even touched her."

"One, I have no bloody idea what you're talking about. Two, it didn't matter if I was right next to her, they attacked us all at first. Burned her arm. Made her see her worst memories. Something about the last time she died.

Three, you're like a freaking toddler—how the hell do you know this shit?"

Ian's brow furrows in confusion for a hot second before understanding dawns. "You two have no idea what you really are, do you?"

I guess not.

CHAPTER ELEVEN

MAX

Sure, she's half-demon, but with an angel in the mix, they wouldn't have even touched her...

I know that voice, but it takes a minute for it to come to me. Ian. Why do I hear Ian? Where in the holy frick and frack am I? My eyelids take their sweet ass time opening, and it takes a while for me to realize I'm looking at the high ceiling of an apartment.

Then the pain makes itself known in a big fucking way, and I have to focus on the world around me, so the white-hot agony of healing bones and closing cuts doesn't take my breath away. The raised male voices grate on my nerves, but I'll take it.

Well, until Ian's words actually filter through my brain.

Sure, she's half-demon... Then, another little gem. *You two have no idea what you really are, do you?*

This has me popping up from whatever the hell it is I'm lying on like a jack in the box.

My voice is made of broken glass, but I manage to croak, "Who's half-demon?"

I can't really pay attention to the answer to my question due to the fact the white-hot agony I felt earlier has now morphed into some sort of soul-searing, mind-bending form of torture, and I nearly pass out. I also vaguely realize that I'm naked as a jaybird from the waist up, a fact I'm not even remotely fond of, but I can't quite process that right now. What I can process—and it's freaking me the fuck out—is the thick tubing coming from my ribs. It's sutured in such a way that my skin puckers around it.

I don't think I'm supposed to be awake for this part of healing. I think humans have it right and comas are probably best for all involved. Yes. A coma would be really nice right now.

"Jesus Christ, Max!" Ian moves in my direction and reaches for me, reclining me back down to what I now realize is a pool table before rummaging into his bag. I hope he has some really good drugs in there because I don't think Ibuprofen is going to cut it.

At this point, I'd take a hammer to the head and suffer through the brain damage. Plus, there is a wounded animal somewhere in this room. The sound coming from it chills me to the bone.

"I'm gonna take care of you." His dark eyes meet mine for a moment before he moves back to rummaging through his bag. It's then that I notice that sort of keening whimper is coming from my throat. I'm making that horrible sound.

"You're going to be fine, baby. I promise."

I feel a needle stick in my arm, and it takes less than a count of two before I'm off in floaty land.

It's then that I realize that no one answered my question, but I don't think I really need them to. I'm pretty sure the answer is something that has plagued me for nearly four centuries.

A truth I never wanted to admit to myself.

If I had a guess, I'd go with the half-demon is me.

But that could be the drugs talking...

I WAKE UP AGAIN IN THE PLUSH SOFTNESS OF A well-made bed. The room is dark, likely the middle of the night. Gingerly sitting up is my sole focus, and I manage to accomplish it without the blistering agony from before. Also, I'm clothed in a black T-shirt and blue boxer briefs. The tube is gone, and it is one of the few things I can mark in the win column.

This is the second time in forty-eight hours I've been dressed by someone *not* me, and I'm finding it rather irritating.

Disembarking the monster of a bed is next, and while I'm not a small woman, the distance from the surface to the floor seems a bit steep. I manage it, though, taking my best guess as to where the bathroom is and handling my business. At this point, I'd kill for a toothbrush, but I make do with the mangled toothpaste tube on the messy counter and my finger.

Then I peruse the bandages on my arms that seem to have gotten bigger, not smaller. That doesn't look good.

I take a gander at myself in the mirror and decide I've definitely looked better. My tan skin has a solid sallow look to it, and the bags under my eyes are big enough to go backpacking around Europe. Plus, my hair is a complete disaster of snarls, dried blood, and Fates know what else.

I need a shower. I need a day off. I need a vacation.

Melody. *Oh, god.*

Tearing out of the bathroom, I open the bedroom door and smack into a tall man in a beanie. I know this tall man, though.

"Who wears a beanie in July?" I stare at Aidan, and it all comes flooding back. I was hurt. Striker must have brought me to Ian.

"Don't judge me for my fashion choices, and I won't judge you for yours, Smurfette."

"Real original. Where's Striker? And Ian? Ian was here, right?" My recollection of events is a little vague.

"In the living room trying not to kill each other, most likely."

I move past him before his words actually register. "Wait, why would they be trying to kill each other?"

Aidan just shakes his head and mutters something along the lines of, "not my circus, not my monkeys."

I make my way down the sparsely decorated hall to an open-concept large room that seems to serve as a living, dining, and kitchen area. It's decked out in a Spartan-meets-frat-boy style. A pool table instead of a dining one, a leather couch that looks like it could seat fifteen, a TV bigger than some billboards, and an entertainment center with every single gaming console known to mankind spilling from it.

If I didn't know them better, I would assume Ian and Aidan were twenty, not over a hundred.

"You'll go in there over my dead, rotting corpse." Ian's low, rumbling growl sounds through the open room.

Ian's standing in Striker's way, a clawed talon pressing into the center of Striker's chest. Striker is holding one of my overnight bags with what I hope is all of my makeup, hair supplies, and a fresh set of clothes, and shoes. For some reason, he isn't letting Striker pass.

"Is there a magic word my best friend needs to say to get past you, or what? Because we can leave. In fact, leaving sounds like a fine option. I got shit to do."

Both men turn to me, Ian's phase fading away before I catch his eyes, but I don't miss the sliver of hurt in them before he masks it.

"I wanted to get you up and dressed so we can go, and Dr. Moran here didn't feel up to releasing his patient while he spewed a bunch of bullshit. But you're awake now, so the argument is moot."

A growl erupts from Ian, but I talk over it.

"Spewed what bullshit?"

"I don't—"

I cut him off before he can give me some excuse. "What bullshit, Striker?" His tawny eyes glow for a second before they narrow, his jaw clenching in that way of his that means he won't tell me unless I beat it out of him.

Striker won't say, but Ian will. "Cough it up." I pierce Ian with my stare. He's all too willing to oblige.

"You're half-demon. Your friend here is half-angel. I don't know what you stumbled in, but those burns on your arms are part of it."

This doesn't throw me for the loop I thought it would —to have it all but confirmed.

"And you're sure about this?" I cross my arms despite the nagging ache in them.

"Pretty sure. I got it from a rather reliable source." Ian mirrors my stance as he gives Striker his back.

"What I want to know," Aidan interjects from behind me, "is what you meant by 'the last time she died.' Are you a necromancer or something?"

His questions sting. It isn't the first time it's been asked, and likely won't be the last.

"No, I'm not a fucking necromancer. I'm not in service to a damn demon. And you two should know what he meant by that. You were both there." I fling out a hand in anger, causing the lights to flicker some. *Whoops.*

"At Mena's. When the ward broke. I didn't save you, did I? I didn't keep you alive. You died." Ian's pained murmur causes my chest to ache.

"If it makes you feel any better, I didn't think I'd come back that time." My voice nearly peters out. "I'd never died that way before, so your efforts were appreciated."

Ian looks at me like I've lost my damn mind, and Striker's eyes start glowing again. Way wrong thing to say.

"No, it doesn't make me feel any better!" Ian scolds. "Why didn't you tell anyone?"

How could I condense a lifetime of pain, suffering, and general despondency into a single sentence?

"I was kicked out of my coven at fourteen for coming

back after being burned at the stake. I have emotional damage. Excuse the shit out of me."

Ian just rolls his eyes. "I'm a half-black Irishman who also happens to have been born over a hundred years ago. Not to mention, I'm also half-wraith and half whatever the bloody hell my mother was to create the amalgamation of abilities that seem to screw me over at every turn. No, I couldn't possibly know what discrimination looks like." His voice is straight deadpan as he blinks at me like I'm an idiot, the Irish in his accent flaring.

Okay, he has a fair point on a multitude of levels.

"So, I should have told you. Agreed. I apologize for withholding pertinent information about myself."

Both Ian and Aidan seem to ponder on my apology for a minute while Striker seethes. I get it. Melody is in the hands of the very men we vowed to protect her from. Getting a move on would be awesome at this point.

"You said everything had to do with Max's burns. You going to elaborate?"

"I can't. I don't know enough about it to say either way. But there's someone we can talk to, and he could help to get your girl back. But if I were you, I'd get dressed up."

"Why?" The question falls from my lips.

"Because we're going to Aether."

I can't figure out why that name sounds familiar until it dawns on me. It's the witch club we went to ages ago.

I hope Striker packed something good in that overnight bag. *I think I'm gonna need it.*

CHAPTER TWELVE

MAX

It took over an hour for me to get my shit tight enough to attempt to walk back into that club. I likely wasn't actually welcome in Aether, but Ian promised us he knew the owner, and could get us in. Luckily, Striker either already planned on going there to ask questions, or he grabbed the first outfit he thought would make me feel pretty after almost getting dead.

I choose to believe option two when it's probably more like option one.

I fidget, pulling the sleeve of my black leather jacket further down to cover the white of the bandages on my forearms as I inspect myself in the lone floor-length mirror in Ian's apartment. Getting ready for a club night isn't my normal, but since my day-to-day look is full makeup and hair, I'm a pro at making myself up in a hurry. Striker helped by drying my rolled hair while I did my eyeliner, so my typical hour and a half get-ready time was cut significantly.

I paired the jacket with a black deep V-cut, loose-fit silk tank and cropped black leather pants. The kicker was the Christian Louboutin five-inch, silver studded, spike-heeled pumps. They are shiny and a little dangerous. I love them, even though the price tag was fourteen steps past ridiculous.

My thick, blue glam waves make me feel a little more normal, even if my whole life is more than a little upside down. Plus, I feel weird. Not sick, not hurt, just weird. Drained, maybe?

"Are you going to look at yourself in the mirror a bit more or are you going to get a move on?" Striker asks from my left as he adjusts the cufflinks of his starched white shirt. He's dressed in a suit again, even though he likely could get away with the outfit he was wearing an hour ago. Like me, he doesn't want to risk getting thrown out before we know something substantial.

"Get a move on, I guess. I feel weird, though."

"You just had a tube in you, draining blood from vital organs. I'd feel weird too. Now, let's go."

Nodding, I follow him to meet Ian and Aidan in the living room. Aidan gives me a wolf whistle, and Ian elbows the taller man in his ribs. No idea what that's about.

Since he's supposed to take us where we need to go, everyone puts a hand on Aidan. Aidan is a full-blooded wraith, and unless his position has changed, he's a guardian for the crowned king and queen of his species. His abilities are a bit of a mystery to me, but the one I'm familiar with is the one where he can smoke in and out of anywhere at any time. One second he's a man, and the next he's a swath of black smoke and gone. It's creepy as hell. Without so much as a count to three, the wraith uses his gifts to transport the lot of us to the Denver warehouse district.

Aidan's wraith gifts are made of suckass, I think as I wobble on my spike heels and try not to vomit on the cracked pavement when we land. Transport the wraith way kind of feels like every molecule in your body is being ripped apart and put together wrong. I am not a fan.

I manage not to lose the contents of my stomach on the sidewalk and follow the men to the warehouse door that seems to have sprung up out of nowhere. Ian slides it open to reveal much the same as the last time I was here. This time, however, the acrobats are on rings suspended from the ceiling that seems to match the starry night sky, and instead of being naked, their bits and pieces are barely covered in peacock feathers. They swing and twirl above the dance floor, and I'm amazed for a second, before my hand is tugged and I stumble forward.

Ian has my hand in his, and instead of flowing around the crowd, we're skirting it completely to find a less crowded section and a solid black door that reads, "Management." Ian knocks, and a woman I recognize opens it. She's tall and blonde, and I distinctly remember her plastering herself on Striker's lap the last time we were here.

"Doctor Moran. I don't recall inviting you. Do you have an appointment?" Her Australian accent curls around her words in a seductive way I don't really appreciate.

This isn't a woman who is unaware of her assets. No, she uses them like a weapon. Her wide blue eyes have a fake innocence to them that I know all too well, and paired with her outfit, I'm pretty sure I have her pegged.

She's wearing a woman's loose-cut tuxedo jacket, but she's missing the blouse underneath. Coupled with a cropped pair of tux pants, and a collared necklace that looks like it's made of golden feathers, this woman knows exactly how she sounds and how she looks. Not that I hate that about her, in fact, I'm dying to know where she got that necklace.

"You and I both know I don't need an appointment, Ruby. Please tell him I would appreciate an audience."

"Very well." She sighs before closing the door. A minute later it opens wide to reveal a long hallway filled with bookcases stuffed to the brim. Every row has its fair share of books. The hallway opens up to what appears to be a library office. The ceiling and walls do not seem to fit in a warehouse but more appropriate inside an opulent mansion somewhere in Europe.

Given the nature of the club, that is totally in the realm of possibilities. The hallway doesn't have even half as many books as the wall-to-wall bookcases that are only sparsely interrupted by a fireplace here and a wet bar there.

A man sits behind a rather sumptuous mahogany desk. I remember this man, too. He's the dangerous, yet attractive guy I saw Striker talking to. His brown hair is swept back from his face as if the strands themselves are too obedient to move out of place. His eyes are a piercing vibrant blue, at odds with his dark hair. At this point I'm glad I put on makeup, since these two are ridiculously gorgeous in a way that has me feeling like a troll.

"Ian, Aidan, Striker. Pleasure to see you. And who is this?" Caim inclines his head to me.

"Caim," Ian nods, "I would like you to meet Maxima Alcado."

I try not to cringe at the use of my full name, but my eye twitches, anyway. This seems to amuse Caim, and a half-smile emerges on his full lips.

"And why have you brought a Rogue into my establishment?" Caim pins me with his steely eyes. They seem to have an X-ray quality I'm not at all comfortable with.

"We have a demon problem." Ian tightens his grip on my hand just a shade.

"Obviously." Ruby stares at me as if I'm a cockroach she is considering stomping on with her pointy-toed shoe.

"While I can see you haven't heeded my advice, what would make you think that I'd help you?"

"Because an incubus attacked an angel, and I was under the impression that was against the Armistice. I kind of thought you'd want to know."

Ian's bold statement seems to catch him by surprise, his eyes widening a mere fraction before he schools himself. Caim manages not to appear ruffled as he steeples his fingers.

"Interesting. That is a very serious accusation."

"It is if what Ian claims is true. That I am somehow half-angel without my knowledge. I believe he got that information from you, and since I've known you for several years, I wonder why I didn't know this."

"One, you didn't ask. Two, I'm not quite sure what your lineage is, I just know that you are most definitely not an empath, and if I had a guess, I'd say you were a seraphim of some sort. Maybe? You're definitely angel mixed with something. But... Your parents are not registered on my list, so I can't say for certain." He shrugs at this, as if informing someone that their entire life has been a lie is no skin off of his nose.

"What list?" Striker sputters. "What registry?"

"I keep the lists of all Ethereals—the ones registered with the Council, anyway. Like you, Maxima Alcado—daughter of witch, Teresa Alcado, and the demon, Andras. But you already knew you were a little different, didn't you? What, with the dying and coming back to life and all? What is it, one hundred and thirty-eight now?"

"One hundred and thirty-nine, and if you would be so kind, please call me Max."

"A demon with manners. How intriguing." Ruby sneers from her perch on the side of Caim's desk.

"Oh, don't listen to Ruby, she's just prejudiced. Plenty of demons have manners. Plenty of angels are outright scoundrels. What we are does not dictate what can be. Ethereals, just like humans, are inherently neutral. Just like me."

"Good to know I won't turn into a murdering psychopath. I was worried there for a minute," I joke, my wry smile mirroring Caim's. "Just so you know, those one hundred and thirty-nine times I've died? Those were because I was helping people. I've never, not in four hundred years, taken a single innocent life. Not one. I would appreciate it if you didn't look at me like I was scum on the bottom of your shoe. The only reason I'm

Rogue is because I came back to life after I was burned at the stake at fourteen."

Ruby appears contrite for a second before muttering, "Shitty," under her breath. She gives me a commiserating nod. I'm not the only one with a shitty past, I guess.

"Give me the particulars of your situation, and I will be happy to see to your claim."

Striker tells him every detail, starting from the tattoo shop, to my home, to the Danvers' farm in Indiana. He doesn't seem surprised except for once, when he learns that they infiltrated my home. Caim nods, makes notes on a legal pad as he listens.

A waitress comes in the middle of Striker's story, supplying Caim with a fresh cup of tea. I meet her gaze for a second. I vaguely recognize her as the waitress who served us, but she was much happier then. Now, her face is pale as a sheet. Ruby dismisses her, and she scurries off, but not before she gives me one last haunted look.

"I'll get this squared away very soon. In the meantime, I suggest you try to locate your Melody using any bit of skin you have touched her with. Try and flex those angel powers of yours, Striker. You'll be surprised what you can do. And Max? You have temporary access to my club, and I'll look into your Rogue status. Your mother is a prickly one, isn't she?"

He doesn't even know the half of it.

I give him my best wry smile, not disparaging her in mixed company, but not denying it, either. My mother is the freaking worst, but I don't know Caim well enough to know if I could speak freely about her to him.

I'm untrained, not stupid.

I simply shrug, and Ruby leads us out of the office and back to the raucous club filled with revelers. I don't make it two steps past the threshold before someone grabs my forearm. I hiss in pain as I yank my arm away from the waitress from before. Her corn-silk-blonde hair is slightly disheveled, her skin sallow with fear.

"I know where your friend is. The pregnant one. She was here. In the basement of the club. I saw her."

She must see disbelief on my face due to the fact she grabs my arm again, making me hiss in pain.

"She was here. I swear!"

But I believe her, and the sheer rage I feel makes it easy to blow Caim's office door to pieces and stomp inside.

He'll look into it, my fabulous ass.

CHAPTER THIRTEEN

MAX

It hits me about ten seconds after I blow the door that my actions may be classified as rash. But given the sheer amount of shit I've gone through to protect Melody only to have her held captive in the very club where we chose to select help, I prefer to overlook it. It probably doesn't help that I'm also dragging a waitress by her arm down the hall to give Caim a piece of my mind.

There are not-so-quiet murmurings at my back, but I'm pissed enough that I don't focus on them.

At the mouth of the corridor in between Caim and me stands Ruby. I'm smart enough to know that I cannot possibly best her in combat, but I'm also dumb enough to test out my abilities on her.

"Everyone needs to calm down and take a fucking seat," I command, my voice thunderous. When I snap my fingers, Caim parks his ass in his sumptuous leather wing-back, and Ruby seems to fly back through the air, landing in a rather comfortable-looking club chair. I hear feet shuffling behind me, and I have to assume it's my friends caught in the same spell.

Well, that is unfortunate, yet, probably for the best.

At this point, Caim appears mildly ruffled, but Ruby is probably contemplating on how best to remove my head from my shoulders. Which is fair.

"Now. We are going to discuss this calmly and rationally, because contrary to popular belief, I don't actually enjoy making enemies. Your lovely waitress overheard our conversation and claims that a woman fitting Melody's description was in the basement of this club. Today. Which means at some point in the last twelve hours you have had a kidnapped pregnant woman in your establishment. Now, I'm all for an errant coincidence, but this smells fucking foul. Care to explain?"

Caim's eyes narrow as his face reddens, and it occurs to me that the only reason everyone is silent is due to the spell I cast. I may have put a little too much juice into that one.

Whoops.

I snap my fingers again. "Sorry," I mutter. It may sound like an afterthought, but I really mean it. If Caim and Ruby have nothing to do with this, then I most definitely don't want to be on their bad side.

If they are, however, I may have just bitten off way more than I can chew.

"In my club?" Caim fumes—his words sound like the faint hiss of a snake right before it strikes. "I want to know exactly what happened, and I want to know exactly where you saw her. Tell me, Silver. No harm will come to you for telling the truth."

The waitress, Silver, shakes in my grip, but I'm hesitant to loosen my hold. If she bolts, I've lost my witness.

"T-there was a man in the back room talking to the new bartender—Vincent? Victor? I don't know his name. Umm... They were arguing about something I didn't hear. But when I went to the stock room to make sure there was enough cocktail napkins before my shift, I heard a wo-woman, and she was crying and screaming. So... I f-followed the sound, and the basement didn't look like our basement, you know? There were people down there, and they were packing up stuff and shoving people in cages. There was a pregnant woman, she was screaming that she wouldn't go, and they hit her in the mouth and she f-fell." Her voice breaks as she covers her mouth.

"Th-they just shut the door on her. I made a noise, and someone was coming to look for me, so I just went back to work, you know? I wanted to tell someone, but it didn't make any sense, and then I thought I'd imagined it, or if I didn't, then I needed to get out of here and never come back. I just-just didn't know if I was gonna get killed because I saw too much." Silver shrugs as she wipes her nose with the back of her forearm. She's still shaking, but somewhere in the middle of her story, I wrapped an arm around her shoulders.

"Can you show us?" I can tell Caim's trying not to snap his desk in half as he asks the question. He didn't do this. No way. If he did, then he deserves an Oscar.

Silver nods and burrows herself under my arm. Poor girl. She's shivering her ass off in her next-to-nothing outfit of some sort of mesh and peacock feathers, so I shrug out of my jacket and drape it over her shoulders.

"Maxima, this will go a lot faster if you would give me back the use of my fucking body," he reminds me.

Shit. I snap my fingers again, allowing everyone to move, mumbling another contrite "Sorry."

Caim sweeps past us, stealing Silver from me and tucking her under his arm as he leads us out of his office. I'm the last one out except for Ruby. As we cross the threshold, I snap my fingers again, turning the obliterated door back into the solid black surface it once was.

Ruby says nothing, but her raised eyebrow tells me volumes—up to and including that she'd really like to wring my neck right about now. I can't do much about that, but I still give her a repentant smile and follow the men to the back of the club. I missed most of this the last time I was here, but I get the feeling the nightclub changes quite frequently.

I catch Striker's blond waves in the crowd and Ruby, and I haul ass to catch up, following them down turns and hallways until finally catching up to them in a secluded back corridor that seems to go on forever. We can't even hear the music from the club or feel the bass of the speakers.

"Ruby, if you would be so kind, secure Vaughn from behind the bar. I have a feeling we'll need to find out exactly what he knows." Caim eyes the door to what I assume is the basement. Ruby nods, and she's gone before my eyes can track it.

Impatient, Striker tries to move past us to get to the door, but Aidan and I manage to grab him by the scruff and yank him back.

"What the shit are we waiting on?" he growls.

"This door does not belong here. The door to my basement is at the end of the hall. This door"—He punctuates his words with a finger point—"goes somewhere else, much like my office does. Since I didn't make the Fate's forsaken thing, I'm checking to see if there are any traps. If you want to get dead because you're too impatient, be my guest. If not, then shut the fuck up and let me work."

I wonder if I should speak up and let him know there isn't warding around the door, but my mouth makes the decision for me.

"There aren't any hex lines. It looks just like your door. The magic is a little cruder but similar. No traps," I mutter as I inspect the door.

Caim stares at me like I've grown another head.

"What? Am I not supposed to be able to see hex lines?"

Caim just blinks at me. I guess not.

He gestures for me to open the door, and despite Ian's growled warning, I actually do it. When nothing happens, I start down a rickety set of stairs and turn the corner to a nearly empty basement. Striker's thunderous footsteps follow me, but his growl in frustration is the real kicker.

We missed them. Detritus of the space being recently used is everywhere. Dirty bare mattresses mixed with the smell of piss and shit, food wrappers, and trash. It smells to high heaven, but no one is left.

Caim seems to churn in his own blind fury as I try to get a glimpse of warding or clues of some kind. I try and fail. The place has been wiped of anything of value. Soon, we all flee the scent of despair and human waste and head back upstairs.

By the time we get there, Ruby is on her way back, and she's frog-marching a young man in front of her. He's shirtless and pretty in that dumb, single-dimensional way that only seems to come from too much magic, too much recreational drug use, or too few brain cells. Based on the somewhat vacant expression on his face, maybe all three.

"Vaughn?" Caim prompts, but he doesn't get a response. Vaughn is vacantly staring down the hall, a floaty unbothered expression on his face.

This smells fishy. No, literally. Magic like this smells like dead fish to me. But not everyone can smell and see magic like I can, I'm guessing.

"Someone jacked with his brain." I gag at the smell. "Forgetting spells smell like rotting fish."

Now *everyone* is looking at me like I grew another head. What?

"You can smell magic, too?" Caim's brow furrows, the question not really a question. His eyes pierce me in that way I'm not comfortable with again.

"Some. Not all. But memory-fudging ones are especially repugnant." I try not to inhale the stench and fail. "Oh, my god, could you put him downwind or something?"

"Can you fix it?" Ruby asks, and I'm tempted to give her the real answer.

On the one hand, this dude is more than likely a member of a black-market smuggling ring of some kind, so fuck him. On the other, I don't know that for sure, so I can't just hand him over to almost certain torture. Plus, just because I get something from him doesn't necessarily mean he'll be all there when I'm done. It's more like deciding if we want his brain fried or scrambled.

Either way, the yolk ain't going back in the egg.

"It depends on what you mean by fixed. With something this bad, this crude? I could pull his last few memories before he was wiped, but there is no real fixing it. His brain is either going to be a vacant mess or a drooling mess. So, unless you want to kill him or get him the best possible care, I don't want to mess around in his noodle too much more than it's already been messed with."

"He's a part of this, get what you can out of him," Caim orders, and I reluctantly do as I'm told.

Muttering in a bastardized version of French Creole, I whisper the spell I learned from a pair of ancient grimoires last year as I touch two fingers to Vaughn's forehead. In the next second, images and emotions flood my mind, flashing and melding together.

Blackness, fear, mixing drinks, anxiety, getting ice from a bar back, anger, arguing with Micah, walking down a hall and down a staircase, being horrified at what is in the basement... nothing... nothing...

"Shit!" My eyes squeeze shut to try and glean a little bit more information. "He was part of this, but he didn't know... He was horrified when he saw what was going on in the basement. Micah was using his house as a base of some sort but didn't tell him what for. Paid him money, but Vaughn didn't ask questions. That basement is really in a home in Provo, Utah."

When I open my eyes, Ruby is holding Vaughn up, his limp body in her arms as blood trickles from his nose and eyes. Oh, no. Vaughn wasn't innocent, but he wasn't evil, either. I didn't mean to hurt him. Yeah, I knew it was a possibility, but...

Tears well in my eyes as Ian throws an arm around my shoulders. I don't know how I feel about Ian being the one to comfort me for killing a man, but at this point, I'll take it.

"Like you said, babe. He was part of this, and there was no way to save him," Ian whispers in my ear as he runs a warm hand up and down my arm.

"Yeah, well, then why do I still feel like shit?"

"You're a good person. Duh." Ruby grunts as she hefts Vaughn into a fireman's carry before discarding his body in a doorway I didn't realize was there. "I'll come back for him. Unless one of you wraiths are hungry?"

"He's not appetizing, but thank you," Aidan diplomatically supplies, and I know what that means. He wasn't evil. Wraiths only eat the souls of the evil.

Shit, now I feel worse.

"There are matters to discuss, ladies and gentlemen. I

suggest we retire to my office to hash them out. And Max?" Caim turns to me.

"Yes?"

"Next time, knock."

I doubt I'll be living that one down anytime soon.

CHAPTER FOURTEEN

MAX

For some reason, Caim's office seems much smaller when we file back into it. I don't know if it is Caim's anger that fills it, or if it is Striker's wrath. Either way, the air is decidedly unfriendly.

Ruby took the liberty of ordering us some food, and while I know it's been ages since I've eaten, I can't seem to make myself take a single bite of the juicy hamburger and fries I requested. Typically, I can eat my weight in burgers. Fries are never turned away, and top it all in guacamole and hot sauce, and you have yourself one ravenous witch. But right now, I just can't make myself eat.

Odd.

I look over at Striker, and even though he hasn't eaten too much in the last twelve hours either, his plate is full, too. The penny-pinching, miser part of myself wants to slap the shit out of both of us for wasting food. Too many times have I been without to be wasteful, but I just can't do it.

Abandoning my plate, I sidle up to Striker. He hasn't so much as said a single peep since we got back to Caim's office. Not that I can blame the man. His world has officially been tossed on its ass.

"Hey, Strike." I rest a comforting hand on his arm. Striker and I have always been kind of touchy—probably from a lack of real families growing up. We needed that comfort from someone, and when we became friends, that comfort came from each other.

But right now, my touch is not welcome. I realize this about a millisecond after my hand makes contact. Striker's shoulders seem to lock, his jaw solidifying to solid granite, and I don't think he realizes it's me before he grabs at the arm attached to the hand touching him—grabs and squeezes with all of the incredible strength and supernatural juice he can possibly manage.

Were I able to get my body to move faster than my brain, I probably wouldn't be in the agony I'm in right now. But alas...

My scream is silent. Striker's is not.

He squeezes out a "don't fucking touch me" through gritted teeth before his body turns and his eyes widen, and he finally lets me go. When his fingers fall away from my still-gauze-wrapped forearm, I feel the blood rushing back into the limb. Then red begins to stain the cotton, and that's when everyone moves.

Somehow, Ian and Aidan are between me and Striker. Ian is in his face—fang and talons at the ready to rip Striker a new one. Aidan is at his back prepared to haul him out of there if need be. Ruby and Caim are behind Striker, and their eyes are all glowy and luminescent— doing the same thing that Striker's do when he's pissed— which he is right now due to Ian being right in his face, threatening some sort of disembowelment with a red-hot poker.

Huh. I guess Striker, Caim, and Ruby are a little more alike than I initially realized.

Silver seems to have hidden somewhere, and here I am bleeding on Caim's Persian rug.

Ian coming to my defense, I don't precisely get—well, I can gather a fucking guess, but I still don't understand why he's doing it. Ian and I have never really gotten along. In fact, the first time I met him, I'd just gotten into a car accident after being rammed head-on by a pair of blood-thirsty werewolves after springing my girl Nicola from a hospital.

I got knocked out for most of the action, but when I

came to, Ian was there. I didn't know he was a friendly, so I blasted him with a dose of magic.

He's hated me ever since.

Or so I thought.

"I do realize tensions are high, but I'm ruining what is likely a forty-thousand-dollar rug, so if someone could help me, that'd be great," I half-shout to be heard over the posturing and male fucking ego.

My words have the desired effect, and Ian stands down, turning back to check my arm. He pulls me over to a pair of leather club chairs and gets to work on me.

"Rancid piece of shit." Ian peels back the tape to look at the wound. I've never really looked at the burns Micah left on my skin, preferring to keep the contents of my stomach right where they were. But since I haven't eaten in a while, the likelihood that I'll chuff is low, so I reluctantly take a gander at the damage.

It doesn't look anything like I thought it would. Sure, it's a burn, but it isn't raised flesh and bubbling skin. It's bloody and isn't healing, but it doesn't look like any burn I've ever seen. Instead, it is a design—a marking burned into my skin, obscuring the tattoo underneath. It looks like two linked crescent moons with an arrow flowing through it. There are cubes and triangles inside triangles, dots and dashes. It's simple yet intricate, like some of the dot and line tattoos that I've done on a few college kids who've pulled a random design from some website.

"That's new," Ian remarks, and the way he does it makes my skin crawl. He knows more than he's saying, and in no way, shape, or form is that good for me.

"Here, I got your bag." Aidan stands beside us, dropping a black duffle at Ian's feet. It takes a second for me to realize he went back to Ian's apartment to grab his med supplies in the time it took me to internally analyze and freak the fuck out over this burn.

A part of me already knows what it is. I don't know what it means, but I know it's really bad.

I want Ian to reassure me. I want him to read the freak-out in my mind and tell me that everything will be okay—that I'm fine. But Ian can't read my mind at all. He can't possibly know that despite my stony expression, I am a jittering fucking mess inside.

Striker is the one who is supposed to know this, but when I glance up from the markings on my skin to the room around us, he's already gone.

Him being able to sense everyone's emotions in a room this small, plus Melody being gone... I get it. I do. I totally understand why he did what he did, why he doesn't want to be touched and why he lashed out. Granted, I wish it hadn't been at me, but I can see his side.

But then again, I don't see it at all. He fell for Melody

in the blink of a freaking eye, and while I'm not one to judge, I'm still shocked that the former man-whore of the Ethereal fell so hard so fast for a woman he barely knows.

What I also can't get is him leaving. Never, not once, have I ever abandoned Striker in the middle of some shit, and there have been many a shit storm in our past. I've been bleeding or damn near dying, or hell, actually dying, and I've never left him.

Dick.

Ian takes his time, cleaning the wound and rewrapping it to give it a chance to heal. The fact that it isn't healing is another concern altogether. I have died and come back in less time than it's taking this stupid burn to heal. When he finishes with the bleeding forearm, he switches to the other, checking the skin for infection, he says. I know it's bullshit.

He wants to know if the other burn is a design, too. It is.

I think I had a little hope before Ian pulled that gauze back. Like maybe it was a fluke, or I was high on adrenaline and shitty situations and my mind made it up.

No such luck.

I turn my mind back to Striker and his problems, seriously not wanting to deal with my own right about now.

"What do you think Striker's mixed with?" I blurt, Ian's head coming up in surprise at the question.

"Why do you ask?" Ian's voice is wary for a second, but I don't know why.

"Well, because it isn't like him to fall this hard, this fast. I was kinda wondering if there might be a biological reason for it, or... I don't know." I shrug. "Like how wraith's mate. What is it? It's the voice, right? You have to hear your mate's voice to trigger it, and then you guys turn into territorial crazy people. Like that. Are there other Ethereals like that?"

Ian just blinks at me for a second, his face like stone. The silence is drawn out enough for me to feel a little uncomfortable before he gives a swift shake of his head and answers me.

"There are a few. Dragons, wraiths, of course, a few species of demon, pretty much any kind of shifter. But each trigger is different, and since we have no idea what he is, other than half-angel, it's anyone's guess."

He doesn't say anything more, his demeanor almost walled-off from me as he collects the detritus of medical supplies in his hands.

Did I say something wrong? Is it rude of me to want to know more about other Ethereals?

Ian gets up to go take care of the blood-soaked gauze and alcohol pads, and Ruby plops down in his vacated chair.

Her face is pensive, her brows drawn in such a way

that I think she's about to tell me I'm about to die. She even opens her mouth only to snap it shut a second later, as she seemingly debates with herself.

"Spit it out, darling, am I dying or something?" I command, exasperated.

Ruby's eyes are pitying, but she shakes her head no. Ian begins to head back to us, and Aidan is somewhere behind me. Striker's gone, and I just can't deal with this shit all at once. Irritated, I pop up from my seat and haul her up with me, stepping away from everyone so I can get whatever she has to say to me out without an audience. We're in the hallway of books before I stop.

"Okay. I'm listening."

"You're not dying, but... you might wish you were. I know we got off to a rocky start, and you might not like me, and I might not like you, but as a sister, you have to know what's on your arm."

"I'm all ears, doll."

"It's a demon brand. A mark of ownership." She's telling me this like she's delivering a terminal diagnosis. And shit, she might be right.

"The demon who branded you, essentially owns you. He can do just about anything to you, against you, and under the Armistice, under the rules of the Council, he has the right. I know you don't have a reason to trust me, but he can do anything to you, and you have no recourse against him."

Right this second, I kind of wish I hadn't abandoned that plush club chair since the ground seems like quicksand ready to suck me up.

"It's how he found me, isn't it? And how he broke my wards?" I ask the question, but I don't really need to. This is so much worse than I thought it would be—to know what that design meant. I thought I was so smart, trying to protect Melody. And who led him there?

Me.

I'm such a freaking idiot.

"Well, thanks for letting me know. Any pointers on how to get it off?"

"There isn't a way to get a brand off, per se. Once it's there, it's there. There is a way to break the brand, and the hold the demon has on you, but it isn't easy."

"Well, sister, I'm all ears. I would fucking love to know how this murdering, woman-beating, human disemboweling, black-market trafficking psychopath can be removed from my life. Please, tell me."

Sure, my voice is snotty, but the answer isn't just yes. The answer is, hell yes. Please, dear god of all that is holy, yes. She raises an eyebrow at me, but, I don't care if I have to hitchhike naked in Antarctica until my tits fall off, I need to break this damn brand.

"You'd have to kill him," Ruby admits, "and killing a demon isn't easy. It's damn near impossible, trust me. But I have a contact you can go to. She's... eccentric, but she knows her stuff. Crones typically have the knowledge the Council refuses to keep or refuses to share."

"The Council?"

"Just a group of old Ethereals who's mission in life is to make rules that no one adheres to. I wouldn't worry too much about them."

Ruby pulls a slip of paper from her back pocket and passes it over.

"Use the information she gives you wisely. Crones don't see good and evil the way you and I do."

What the hell am I about to get myself into?

CHAPTER FIFTEEN

MAX

In the unlikely event I make it out of this mess, I'm going to kill Ruby. Based on her directions—which I really should have read all the way through before embarking on this Fate's forsaken trip—I'm supposed to leave the trailhead located two-point-four miles past the parking lot at Hanging Lake, and make my way down into the valley gorge. At four in the freaking morning.

This must be a joke.

I don't camp. I don't hike. The most outdoorsy thing I do is grow herbs and flowers in a greenhouse and drink wine on my freaking patio.

I also sure as shit do not want to jump into a pitch-black valley from this outlook spot since that is the only freaking way to get there. Oh, and it's the only way to get there because the cliff face is a ninety-degree slope.

Ruby's note specifically says no magic. Well, Ruby and her note can go eat a dick.

There is no other way to get down there besides rappelling off the freaking cliff, and I can't exactly do that in Chucks. It's bad enough I have to walk this path in the pitch-black dark armed only with a backpack full of spell ingredients and a flashlight by myself, since Striker is nowhere to be found.

Yeah, I'm four hundred years old. Yeah, I can take care of myself. But... there are bears and cougars out here. And snakes and creepy crawly...

Fuck it.

I'm not spending one more second out here in the damn dark. Snapping my fingers, I transport myself to the tree-laden gorge. Granted, landing in a stream was not my intended destination, but I'll take the soaked Chucks over almost certain death. I slosh my way out of the stream, snapping my fingers once again to dry my feet.

I should have listened to Ian. *Don't trust Caim and Ruby,* he'd said. Did I listen? Nope. Did I even give him the time of day when he tried to talk me out of this shit? Double nope. I'm the dumbass who said I needed to go to "the bathroom" and freaking left him there. Honestly, I'm no better than Striker.

Survey says? I'm an asshole.

Maybe I'm still reeling from what Ruby said. Maybe I

can't deal with being that close to Ian. Maybe Striker really hurt my feelings. Maybe a little bit of all of the above is making me a little out of sorts.

But hurt feelings aren't going to get this brand off, that is for damn sure. Hopefully, this random-assed trek in the mountains will do that.

Now that I'm down here, I can faintly see the pale-white hex marks surrounding the perimeter of a warded rickety-looking cabin. Smoke wafts from a crooked chimney, filtering through the ward and disappearing off into the night.

I can walk through the ward, but most witches don't like the violation, so I do the only polite thing and knock, touching a tiny bit of magic to the warding lines. I have to be careful, or I'll bust the ward, and then everything will be shot to shit.

It wouldn't be the first time.

The door opens, and, immediately, I'm confused. When Ruby said crone, I half-expected an ancient woman hunched from the years, maybe blind or crotchety or both. Okay, I more than half-expected. But what I get is an elegant lady with silver hair, warm brown eyes, killer eyeliner, and a pretty cocktail ring with a giant aquamarine in the center of the setting.

I only notice the ring when she sweeps her chin-length bangs off her forehead in an old Hollywood-style classic move. It looks equally elegant and likely practiced with the level of effortlessness it takes to look that classy.

"Maxima, darling, do come in," she offers via a posh-sounding English accent. "I've put on a fresh pot of tea, and I have biscuits cooling on the counter." She waves me into her cabin with a flourish of her hand.

After all I've been through, it's tough to not be wary when someone I don't know, knows me, but I suck it up and give her a smile. Outside, the cabin appears to be a one-room shack. Inside, however, it's more like a luxurious cabin mansion. Thick beams span the vaulted ceiling that I know couldn't possibly fit under the piddly offerings of the tiny planked roof.

Magic is a trip. Four hundred years later, and it still catches me by surprise.

The crone ushers me toward a silk damask armchair, a pair of steaming cups of tea sitting on the coffee table in front of it. Its twin sits opposite, and she relaxes into the plush offerings. I feel stiff and formal until the crone picks up her tea, slides off one of her ballet flats and tucks a leg under her, settling in.

"Thank you for your hospitality. I apologize for calling on you so late."

"Oh, it's no bother. I so rarely get visitors. You'd think I'd have cannibal tendencies with the way I've been avoided. I don't, by the way. People just forget, I suppose."

O-kay.

"You know my name, but I don't know yours. I suspect calling you 'The Crone' is a little…"

"Coarse?"

"Yes, that works."

"My name—not that anyone has asked me in some time—is Bernadette. I say this with the caveat that I've had several names over the years. I've lived a very long time. For the sake of our conversation, however, Bernadette will do."

"A pleasure to meet you." I nod. "Did Ruby tell you why I was coming here or…"

"Ruby? That little wench? No. Decidedly not. She and I try to stay as far from each other as possible. I find her and her ilk very irritating." Bernadette waves her hand in dismissal before taking a delicate sip of her tea.

"They can be, but so can anyone. She directed me to you for help. She said you had 'the knowledge the Council refuses to keep or refuses to share.' Now, I don't know anything about a Council, but if you have information that could help me, that would be appreciated."

"While I'm glad she sent you to me, it really depends. What information do you seek?"

I can't help but sigh before I pull back the tape and gauze covering my forearm and show her the brand.

She peers at my arm. "Oh, dear."

"Pretty much. Ruby said you knew how to break a brand."

"Well, of course I can break a brand. You can, too, *if* you do it right, but it isn't the breaking that's the problem, is it? You don't have the right tools. The action is easy, but if you don't have the tools for the job, well, then you're fucked, I suppose."

"Well, by the look of things I'm fucked one way or another. I'd really love to not be fucked by this particular asshole."

Bernadette whips her hand out and latches onto my forearm, inspecting the lines and symbols behind a pair of jeweled reading glasses she pulled from I have no idea where. Her hands have the thin, papery quality of an aging grandmother, but are also imbued with enough strength that I know there is probably no way to get out of her hold.

"An incubus I take it? Parasitic little buggers, aren't they? Oh, dear, he made you see your deaths? Well, that is just rude. No one wants to relive dying." She inspects the lines from one end to the other, practically having a conversation with the information she gleans from them.

"There are two brands, if that information helps."

"It does, let me see."

Pulling back the bandage on the more healed of the

two, Bernadette sucks in a breath as she latches onto the other arm.

"This is not good, my dear Maxima. I need to slow the healing process for these burns. If they heal all the way, there will be no breaking the brand. This is going to hurt, child, but it's the only way to give you a little time. Brace yourself."

I don't think I processed how bad this is going to hurt before she rakes her thumbs over the injured flesh. Breaking the skin, blood wells from both designs running down my arm. Before the drops can reach the plush rug, however, Bernadette snaps her fingers and a silver bowl appears underneath my arms, catching the rich red droplets. A few seconds later, my arms are rewrapped in fresh gauze, but the stinging refuses to go away.

Honestly, I think I might hurl. I can't even hiss in pain, it hurts so bad.

"Okay, okay. I know it hurts. I know, darling girl. Just breathe through it." Her calm voice floats through the fog of agony currently surrounding me. Managing to take some mildly hiccupping breaths, the pain abates a bit. Oh, my god, this is so much worse than when Striker squeezed it.

"All right, doll, we have less time than I thought we did, so you're going to listen to what I have to say and not give me any lip. Deal?"

"I'll make an effort as long as you don't do that again."

"I can work with that. What you want to do—breaking a brand—has consequences. Killing a demon isn't easy, but living after you've done so paints a target on your back. In more ways than one. Trust me on this. You need to decide if this is something you can live with. I know your lineage, dear. Your family's history is rife with turmoil. You, yourself, have been on the receiving end of Fate's cruel hand. This might not be something you can come back from."

"I understand."

"No, dear, I don't think you do, but I've said my piece. Now, you need to stay hidden. I can help with that. You see this ring?" She offers her right hand to me, showing me the large aquamarine cocktail ring. The large oval stone spans nearly the entire length of the base of her finger to the first knuckle. The pale-blue stone glistens from the bulky geometric setting. Line and dot designs along with sigils decorate the thick metal setting and the wide band.

I've seen something similar, yet very, very different in my past. Something a bit larger—a cuff—hid a very troubled woman and stole her mind along with it. But Bernadette is not the woman I knew.

"This ring has kept me hidden—from demon and angel alike—for more than five hundred years. I want you to take it." She slips the wide cocktail ring off her finger and puts it in my palm.

"I couldn't. Don't you need it?" I try to offer it back. Yeah, the ring is killer and would be really freaking nice to have right now, but... I don't want to take something away from a woman who has been nothing but kind to me.

"I think my solitude is about over, don't you?" She plucks the ring from my palm, grabs my right hand, and slides the still-warm metal on my third finger. "You need the blood of a member of his line, the bone knife I gave your mother in 1627—which she never returned by the way—and the spell I gave her. I am not allowed to recreate the spell for another, but it can be passed down if your mother will be willing to part with it."

"You want me to go talk to my mother? *My* mother? You want me to go ask the woman who banished me from my coven and made me a bloody Rogue after being burned at the stake, for a favor?"

Bernadette winces at me before nodding.

Fabulous.

CHAPTER SIXTEEN

MAX

Finding my mother has never been a problem. I've always known where she was. Typically, I use her position in this country—or even on this planet—as a pinpoint of the exact place I do not want to be. We've crossed paths maybe ten times in the last four hundred years, each time somehow, some way to my own detriment. Still, I somehow find that little beacon inside myself a comfort. Despite the way she's treated me, I like knowing my mother is alive somewhere. Even if I want to knock her into next year.

Likely, this attitude will come to bite me in the ass at some point.

My cream and black T-strap heels make tiny puffs of dust as I stroll up my mother's front drive. For some reason after talking to Bernadette, I felt the need to wear my armor to speak with my mother. Decked out in a tight-as-sin, black-and-white polka dot wiggle dress, I feel almost myself. I'm mostly covered from neck to knees except for the dainty cap sleeves and square neckline, but I'm pretty sure my mother will have a problem with it. Likely the tattoos, blue hair, and the general "I don't give a fuck" attitude will cause a stir, too.

I am way too sober for this.

Hell, if I could, I'd have brought a flask and pre-gamed it until I was half-trashed before I set a single toe in Idaho. Unfortunately, Teresa Alcado has the nose of a bloodhound and the capacity for more judgment than a Baptist preacher's wife. I could be wearing nipple pasties and a G-string or a nun's habit, and my mother would probably look at me the same way.

Walking up the drive of my mother's Coeur d'Alene home at six in the morning will grant me exactly zero favors from her, but I can't seem to resist watching her security people lose their freaking minds as I stride right through her wards.

My mother excels at a lot of things—warding around bloodlines is not one of them. She seems to forget that Rogue status or no, we still share blood.

I don't make it to the porch before she whips open the front door of her house, clad in a bathrobe and pajamas. Her bronze skin is just as flawless as I remember it, her dark coffee-colored eyes under expressive black brows all under solid black waves that are pulled up into a messy morning bun. One of those expressive brows arches and I feel about ten years old.

Now, here is the real test of how this could go. She could either shun me from her property —which will not go very well for her security people—or she'll let me in. I'd almost take the shunning at this point so I can avoid the scrutiny of her stare.

I can see her turning it over in her head as she looks me over before her eyes narrow on the bandages on my forearms. I knew I should have worn a jacket.

The silence stretches on and on before she lets out a long-suffering sigh and raises a brow. "Have you had breakfast?" It's like she expects me to lie or something.

"No, ma'am."

"Well, come on in." She steps away from the doorway, and immediately, her security seems to relax.

I give her a sidelong glance as I cross the threshold. "Don't let them relax. I have trouble after me or else I wouldn't be here in your hair."

I walk past her, heading for what I think might be the kitchen to wait for her. Plopping down on a barstool at a rather beautiful marble island, I resist the urge to go in search for a cup of coffee or a bottle of bourbon.

My mother follows me into the kitchen a few minutes later. "Thank you for the head's up."

"No problem."

"Would you like a cup of coffee?" I nod, because, caffeine, and hell, yes. "How do you take it?"

"Black's fine, thank you." She pours the glorious black liquid into a vibrant turquoise mug and passes it over. I'm able to take a single fortifying sip before she starts the questioning.

"Why are you here, Maxima?" That right there is the reason why I loathe my full first name—the way my mother says it like an accusation. Like my mere existence is an inconvenience.

Hell, it probably is for her.

I have to debate with myself whether or not I want to tell her everything. If I don't, she'll try and sniff it out of me. If I do, she can use any little bit of it against me.

For lack of better options, I pick door number two.

"A few days ago, a pregnant woman came into my tattoo shop with her boyfriend. My business partner, Striker, sensed she was in trouble, and we decided to help her. In the middle of trying to get her to safety, we discovered the boyfriend was an incubus. Since I didn't know that demons even existed until three days ago, I was ill-equipped to handle such a situation. In my attempts to get her and

Striker to safety, I was unfortunately branded. Since I have absolutely no intention of being an incubi's plaything, I would like your assistance in the form of the bone knife and spell Bernadette gave you for killing a demon."

By the time I finish with my request, my mother's face has gone from her usual bronze to a sickly white. That can't be good.

"Also, I would love to know why Caim informed me I was half-demon and not you. Granted, I'll take the spell and knife, the information is more of a bonus request."

"Wha... Why didn't Bernadette just give you the spell?" She blows right past my request for information. Granted, I did tell her she could, but I kind of hoped she wouldn't.

"She said she couldn't recreate the spell, but you could pass it down to a relative. Since my Rogue status does not revoke a familial tie, here I am. Plus, you have the knife I need."

"And you want me to give you the only spell in history that can kill a demon?"

"Well, it's either beg you for help or become a demon's plaything. I've seen how this demon plays with its toys, Mother. He does it by disemboweling them. Since I can't exactly die, that means torture over and over again. Forever. And that's if I'm lucky. I think bringing myself here when I knew how I would be received is testament enough. How's this? If I happen to die for real this time, I'll put a rider in my will that you get them both back. Happy?"

"Not even remotely." She crosses her arms. "Where does Caim fit in all of this?"

Oh, I'm in for it now.

"My friend Ian is familiar with him through business and suggested we go to him for help. It turns out the incubus has been running an underground smuggling ring out of Caim's club, and Caim is pissed. I figure I'm not the only person looking for this guy, but I'm the only one with the actual means to kill him. Caim likely won't because of the Armistice, and if I don't get Micah before the wounds heal, I'm screwed."

"That or Caim is getting you to do his dirty work. I wonder what he's getting out of all of this."

"I have no illusions, Mama. I know that Caim is likely getting revenge and using me to do it. The bonus is I won't be a slave to a psychopath. It sounds like a solid win for me."

"Interesting."

"Plus, Caim said he would look into revoking my Rogue status. I think it will be a very beneficial partnership despite the risks."

At that statement, she narrows her eyes. Jesus, here we go. My mother is a lot of things. Power-hungry is at the tippy top of the list. Ruthless is a close second. She has fought tooth and nail to get where she is in this world, and despite our bad blood, I don't want to jeopardize that.

"I don't want your coven, Mother. I know I'm powerful but being in a coven was never going to work for me. I'm too different. You and I both know that. I scare people, and I can't live with people who fear me. I just want a chance to not be alone. To have access to everything I was denied since I was labeled something when I was a child."

"You put us in danger!"

I'm so pissed, the panes in mama's glass-fronted cabinets start to shake. If I don't get a handle on myself, the glass will shatter in three... two... one...

I manage to pull myself back before everything explodes, but not before every single pane of glass is decorated in a spider web of cracks. I can't say I'm sorry about it one bit.

"You made a ward that drove away anything that wasn't a witch and then wondered why I chafed under the strain of it, even though you knew I was half-demon. A demon used me to drop the ward and free himself from the snare. Men saw me, stripped me naked and burned me alive, and what did you do? You cast me out from the only family I ever knew and turned your back on me. Even before then..." I trail off before finding my voice again.

"You refused to teach me anything about being a

witch, so I couldn't protect myself. Even the simplest of spells. Everything I know today, I taught myself, and I still make mistakes because I don't know the basic fundamentals that every single other witch knows. You neglected me and your responsibility as my mother. You did not protect me—or if you did—not in the ways you should have."

I don't want to dredge all of this up, but just the thought that I would be out for her position pisses me off, and I cannot stand her blaming me for my first death.

"Really? I didn't protect you? Okay. So, I didn't keep you away from your father? I didn't hide you under ward after ward so he couldn't find you? I didn't keep you away from the craft so your power wouldn't grow, and he'd be drawn to you like a beacon? I didn't stay your sentence with the coven so they wouldn't try to kill you? No. I didn't protect you at all, did I?"

Now she tells me. This info would have been great four hundred years ago.

"Had you told me any of this, our lives would have been different. How was I to know what was beyond the ward? You wouldn't even look at me. You told me to shut up and sit down and not ask questions. How could I have known the danger? You kept me ignorant and secluded and unloved. Why did you even have me? Why keep me? Even now, you struggle to look at me."

She does. Her chocolate-brown eyes are staring at my forehead, not my face.

"You look like him, okay? You look like Andras." Her voice breaks as she shakes her head. "He never loved me. He used me to make that blade for him. Seduced me. When I fell pregnant with you, I thought we would be a family, but he left on his quest to find the demon he needed to kill. I had you before he came back, and I was so excited to introduce you to him. But when he came back, he wasn't the Andras I knew. He was cold and cruel and used his compulsion on me so I would hide the blade for him. So, I did, I took the blade, and I took you, and we all went to the New World to hide."

"He broke your heart." She nods. "He broke your heart, and you took it out on me."

"Yes." She swipes at the tears under her eyes. "I'll give you the blade and the spell on the condition that you never attempt to overrule my position on this or any other coven."

"Fine."

"Then we have a deal. But I suggest you watch yourself and the people you surround yourself with. Caim has trouble delivering on his promises. Trust me on that."

This makes me more than wonder what in the hell Caim promised my mother.

CHAPTER SEVENTEEN

MAX

Tracking Striker down in a city the size of Denver is not my idea of a good time. Considering the only sleep I've gotten in the last three days has been while I was rendered unconscious due to blood loss, I'm not exactly my usual chipper self. Better known as, if I don't find Striker in this bar, I'm going to go fucking nuclear.

I silently debate the ramifications of said temper tantrum as I inspect the dank façade of the shitty little hole-in-the-wall bar that I'm about to enter. Don't get me wrong, I love shitty little hole-in-the-wall bars, but this would be the thirtieth such bar I've searched in the last sixteen hours, and I'm getting cranky.

I knew I never should have given him that shielding

amulet in the '60s. I knew one day it was going to bite me in the ass.

A part of me wants to go it alone on this. I have just about everything I need to kill Micah —except for his blood of course—but roping Striker in on this might help him get his shit together.

I hope.

I don't particularly enjoy being irritated at my best friend, but right now, I kind of want to kill him a little bit. I've done everything I can to try and find the little shit, but after my third attempt at scrying, my tenth attempt at a locator spell, and kicking in his front door, I quickly realized Striker didn't want to be found. My only option was going door to door to locate his wayward ass.

He's just lucky these pretty shoes are comfortable, or I'll kick him in the nads the next time I see him. Hell, I still might.

I yank open the door, giving it a little elbow grease since the hinges might have been forged the same year I was born, and slip inside. Inside, the smell is stale beer, old cigarette smoke, even though no one has been allowed to smoke in a bar in over a decade, and orange soap. The place is practically empty except for a tired-looking bartender, a drunk couple of men playing a rather pitiful round of pool, and an old man in a corner booth staring at a glass of amber liquor, and Striker.

He's sitting at the bar, his blond head in his hand as he draws lines in the condensation on the bar top with his finger. A sweating tumbler of Scotch sits next to his hand, and the bottle not far from it. If I had a guess, Strike is completely shitfaced.

Goody.

I begin my long-suffering trek to pick up my cargo when the pair at the pool table finally notice my entrance. I understand that I'm beautiful—this fact has never been lost on me. But I'm also a firm believer in look, don't touch—an adage these gentlemen have either not learned or choose to ignore, considering the pair of them are now standing in my way.

They are possibly in their thirties, but hard living and too much alcohol have aged them considerably, stealing their likely once-good looks. One is blond, the other dark. Wedding rings on their fingers glint in the low light.

Their poor wives.

I have a lot of respect for humans. They are typically more aware of their surroundings than other species, and more often than not, they get a trill down their spine when they cross an Ethereal's path. They know to stay away from us.

These two dipshits, not so much.

"Today is not the day, gentlemen," I warn, not in the mood to get into it with them.

The blond one just smirks at me, his sneering half-smile pissing me off so bad I've snapped my fingers before I can even really think about it. The next second he seems to slip on nothing, falling just so, his face smacking the pool table on his way down.

I don't look at him. Instead, I lock eyes with the human barring my way, raising my eyebrow in challenge. His expression has the wide-eyed quality of a frightened child, so I give him a sweet smile.

"Like I said, today is not the day. Move. Or I'll move you."

He moves out of my way, not even bending to help his friend who is still holding his nose, blood seeping in between the gaps in his fingers. The dark-haired one has some brains, I'll give him that. I step over the groaning man, making my way to my drunk best friend.

It takes Striker a solid minute to realize I'm even standing there, and another thirty seconds or so to blink his bleary eyes at me.

"Well, aren't you a sad sack of shit."

"I can't find her, Max." Striker's words come out in a slur. "Looked everywhere, used my powers n'evrthing. Call'd in markers…" He shrugs and takes a swig of his tumbler. "She's just gone. Miss her, Max. She was the first girl I thought I could have something with, you know? I saw her and her pregnant belly, and I wanted that. I wanted a family of my own."

"So, you're giving up then? Okay. I'll just get rid of this spell that makes a demon-killing blade, and we'll drown our sorrows. You, your lost love, and me because as soon as this brand heals, I'll be a demon's plaything. I mean, I have almost everything to defeat the prick, but sure, let's bitch out now."

Striker blinks at me, and my words seem to register because he blinks again, his gaze going from bleary to sharp.

"What did you just say?" His voice is no longer slurred.

"I don't know, it must have slipped my mind after searching for your dumb ass for sixteen hours after you left me at Caim's. I had to go talk to my mother. By. My. Self, you asshole." At each point, I drive one of my well-manicured fingertips into his chest.

"Max, don't fuck with me on this. What did you say?" he demands as he struggles to stand, knocking his stool over in the attempt. As far as intimidations go, I find it somewhat lacking. Especially since he still needs to hold onto the bar to stand.

"I'm not talking about this shit here, so you need to decide if you're done drinking or not." I cross my arms and give him my death stare. I can't believe I had to track him down. I can't believe I had to do all the legwork. I can't believe he abandoned me at Caim's.

What am I, his fucking mommy?

"I'm done."

"You damn well better be. Let's go."

"YOU'RE TELLING ME YOU WALKED THROUGH Teresa's wards, hashed out some emotional family drama, and she just handed over the knife and spell? We are talking about your mother, right? The same one who made you a Rogue in the first damn place?" Striker gives me his most skeptical eyebrow raise as he takes a seat in his terrycloth bath towel.

After the bar, we headed back to the apartment over the shop to hash everything out. Mostly because Striker is not a small man, alcohol and standing for him is not advised, and my upper-body strength is somewhat lacking. I have enough ingredients here for just about anything, so it was just as well. I didn't feel safe going back to my house, anyway. Freshly showered, he seems half-sober, but I trust his sober status about as much as he trusts my mother—meaning, not at all.

"She made me promise not to go after her seat." I shrug with a bit of indifference. I can't quite look at him, though, and that is a red flag if there ever was one.

"Yeah, right. She didn't make you do a vow-binding spell or anything? You honestly think she'll just take your word for it? I don't think so."

"You really think she'd screw me over?" When I ask the question, I mean it for real this time. Am I really an idiot for trusting my mother?

"Yes. Yes, I do. I trust Teresa Alcado about as much as I trust Caim or Ruby. Did you know I've known Caim for more than a century, and this is the first I've heard about being an angel? Ian knew before I did, which means it can't be that much of a secret."

"At least it explains why none of my hangover cures ever worked on you. I was calibrating for the wrong species. Now quit stalling and chug-a-lug. I need you sober before we hash this out."

"I don't wanna. It smells like moldy feet." He pouts and stares at his glass of sickly purple potion with serious trepidation. I agree with him on the smell, but it's his own fault he's still hammered.

"Plug your nose, then. Make it snappy."

Striker's brow furrows as he dutifully plugs his nose and downs it in one long gulp. His face turns a sickly shade of green for a moment, and then he hauls ass back to the bathroom. The retching I hear sounds violent. Oh, well.

A few minutes later, Striker hobbles out of the bathroom sweaty and gray. "Did you poison me? Sweet Jesus." He collapses into the chair with a groan, covering his face with a hand.

"No, but you needed to get the alcohol out of your system. The potion will take care of what's not in your stomach. Should take about thirty minutes or so. I think. I'm not quite sure with angels. Shouldn't you have self-healing abilities or some cool shit at least?"

Striker peers at me through the gap in his fingers before sliding them down his face. "I may have some things up my sleeve that I haven't told you about. I feel bad about it, but..." He trails off with a shrug. "I knew it was weird and I'm not comfortable with them, you know?"

I FORCE MYSELF TO BLINK AND GIVE HIM A reassuring smile, but that admission hurts a little. There is nothing about me that Striker doesn't know.

"I get it."

"You don't get it. I hurt your feelings."

"I can understand where you're coming from and still be hurt that you didn't trust me, babe. It's called seeing both sides. Now go put on some clothes, brush your teeth, and we can get started."

"Bossy bitch," he mutters but gives me a half-smile so

I know he still loves me. He'd better. I don't search the bowels of Denver for just anybody.

"Stubborn asshole."

He smiles for real then, climbing to his feet and heading to the spare bedroom where I keep some clothes for him. I conjure a toothbrush with a snap of my fingers and hear a "thank you" called through the thin walls.

I hate that I didn't know more about Striker. I hate that I probably can't trust my mother. I seriously dislike that Caim and Ruby aren't exactly on the up and up. But more, I want this to work. I want to be able to get the drop on Micah. I want Melody and her baby safe.

I can want all damn day. It's the getting that hasn't exactly been my style. Here's hoping that part of my life is over.

CHAPTER EIGHTEEN

MAX

"I want to go over it one more time." Striker snatches the vial of salt from my fingertips.

"Are you kidding me? We've gone over it ten times already." I snatch the vial back, but I stuff the stopper back in the top.

That's a lie. We've probably gone over the plan twenty times, but the first ten, Striker was still a little hammered, so they don't really count.

He runs his hand through his hair as he winces before pleading, "Just one more time?"

"Fine. What stage of the plan are you unclear on?" Oh, yes, I am in full-on pissy bitch mode complete with my hands on my hips and everything.

Striker purses his lips, giving me the squinty glare I so hate seeing on his face. "The part where we just leave and don't immediately kill him. I'm real fucking unclear on that particular point."

For the love of all that is holy. If I didn't need him on this, I'd just leave him here. "The plan requires us to get his blood, do the spell, and then we can kill him. Do you want him to kill me before I can get the spell done?"

"No," he grumbles.

"You seem torn on that. Are you sure? Because it isn't like I can do the spell with him just standing there. Which means we need to grab the blood and Melody and get the hell out of there. Spell's done, then we can kill him, okay?"

"Fine."

"Striker!"

"I said *fine*."

Right. Like that petulant "fine" meant dick. I swear to the Fates, my eye is actually twitching. He has pissed me off enough that parts of my body are moving of their own accord with zero prompting from my brain.

"Please keep in mind that you killing Micah will start a war. I haven't read this Armistice, but enough people are bitching about it for me to know it's bad news. It doesn't matter what goes down. You aren't killing him. We're going in, getting Melody and his blood, and getting out. Don't screw us over for revenge, Striker."

"I won't!" His tone is adamant, but for the first time, I wonder if I can actually trust my oldest friend.

I give him a long look, trying to figure out if he's even capable of this. All things considered, I could ask Ian instead. I probably should. Then again, he'd more than likely slam the door in my face for leaving him at the club. Which would be fair, I guess.

"Learn a little patience in the next thirty seconds, or I won't take you, do you understand?"

"Fine. Whatever. I'm a pillar of fucking virtue. You and I both know that Melody doesn't have a lot of time, so if you could get over the fact that I'd really like to kill him despite how much it dicks with the plan, that'd be great. I want to, but I won't because that would likely hurt you both. Are you happy now?"

"Immensely." I scale back the snide just a little. He's worried this won't work, and hell, if I'm being honest, so am I.

I draw the circle with salt, muttering a locator spell in Latin, modified a touch so I can use it for my own ends. The magic of the brands currently burned into my forearms have their own power, all I need to do is trace the thread back to Micah. It's an easy enough trail to follow, and I grab Striker's hand, pulling him with me as I transport us there in a flash of green light.

As soon as our feet touch the dew-damp ground, I

know something's wrong. I can't tell you what state we are in or what country, but I know without a doubt my plans have already gone up in a puff of smoke.

Caim said that demons aren't inherently evil, but I'm having a hard time wrapping my mind around it.

Striker and I are on the edge of a two-lane highway. There is a dense forest behind us, but that isn't the worry. The trouble comes from what lies ahead, across the road. Set back off of the highway is a sprawling two-story house, with a wrap-around porch. On that porch is a woman sitting in a rocking chair.

Her shoulder-length blonde hair is cut into a stylish long bob, pair that with her equally stylish slouchy T-shirt and skinny jeans, it's likely she's the owner of this establishment, which appears to be a bed and breakfast. She seems nice. Probably ran the local bake sale to raise money for the church or elementary school. Maybe even ran a carpool or led a Girl Scout troop or something.

It's clear those days are over, because even from this distance, it's shockingly easy to see her throat is cut. Well, cut is the wrong word. Cut would imply that some form of blade was used when more than likely it was claws or talons that ripped her flesh apart.

"Jesus. Fucking. Christ."

I can't help but nod at Striker's words.

"Okay, new plan. Get Melody out and then go. Screw

the blood, the spell, *and* the blade." I don't know why exactly I'm whispering, but I am.

It isn't like this is my first dead body—or even my twentieth—but shit, this whole situation is way less hospitable than I hoped it would have been. I thought, hey, I can totally seduce the dude who originally wanted to get into my pants, right? Then, surprise! Bing, bam, boom, steal a little blood, Striker grabs Melody, and ta-da! We're done.

Murdered B&B owners were not part of the plan.

"Agreed."

The trek across the street and through the yard is one of complete silence, and it's one of the longest walks I've ever taken. I've never been happier in my life to be wearing flat shoes than I am right now. A part of me knows that Micah is in this house, knows that he killed this woman, but the only bright spot in all of this is the near certainty that Micah is alone. But the same section of my brain that has all this information also knows for a freaking fact I'm going to have to run at some point.

Striker pulls ahead of me, going up the porch stairs first to the front door. The poor woman—be she the owner or a patron—has been dead for a few hours at least, based on the amount of congealing blood beneath the motionless rocking chair. In the middle of the largest puddle is a set of keys that I pray we won't have to use.

Striker draws a dagger from the inside of his jacket before he turns the knob. In a stroke of luck, we find the door unlocked, filing inside as quietly as we can. But this house—while beautiful—is probably at least eighty years old. My feet hit a loose board, creating a grating creak that seems too loud for the stillness of this space.

Then, the squeaks of my Vans on the hardwood or the clunky latch on the door don't matter. Because there is a baby crying in this house, a newborn by the sounds of it. I can't stop Striker from following the cries up the staircase or down the hall.

I don't want to follow him, but I do it, anyway. The pit in my stomach grows with every step I take closer to that sound. I've seen too much death at Micah's hands to believe this will all be okay. I'm only an arm's length behind Striker, but when he freezes in the doorway of the far room, I wish I would have protected him better.

I wish I would have gone alone.

Because he makes this grief-filled howl that has tears falling from my eyes before I even know what is going on. I pull him away, shoving him from the doorway, so I'm between him and whatever it is that's making him make that sound.

But what I see, no one should ever have to see.

Micah is there, holding his child swaddled in a bloody bath towel, but that isn't what has me gasping for air.

That is saved for the massacre he has made of Melody. She didn't have this baby naturally, or if she tried, it didn't end that way. The gaping maw of her belly tells the tale well enough. Micah cut that child out of her womb, and by all accounts was just going to leave her there to bleed to death.

I make a decision—which is probably the wrong one, but I don't have the luxury of a real choice—and rush to Melody. Well, I start to, but I don't make it. My feet freeze about three steps into the room, glued to the floor by whatever magical hold Micah has over me.

He comes closer, and for the life of me, I want to snatch that baby from his arms. He doesn't get that child. He doesn't deserve that innocence, that joy he's stolen from Melody. He doesn't.

Micah's eyes flash red, his mouth pulling up into a boyish half-grin.

"I'll come back for you later, Maxima," he taunts. "Maybe when I'm done with you, you'll fare a little better than she did." Then he slides a single finger along my temple and down my jaw, cutting the tender flesh under my chin with his newly formed talon. He shifts even closer, sniffing at the skin of my neck.

"Yes. I'll enjoy making you my pet," he whispers in my ear, and it is everything I feared. That brand is real, the bond that makes it almost impossible to move is real. Ruby didn't make it up, and Bernadette wasn't lying.

He means every single thing he says.

I can't speak, frozen in the horror of every single atrocity committed here today as Micah just smokes out of the room, leaving the smell of blood and sulfur behind him. As soon as he's gone, my body relaxes for half a moment before I'm ripping off my zipped hoodie and pressing it to Melody's middle.

"M-my b-baby. He t-took my baby," Melody stutters as her body is wracked with shivers from blood loss. Her lifeblood soaks her ripped maternity top and leggings and the bedding around her.

"We're gonna find him, baby. We are." Striker helps calm her, appearing at my side. I can't fix this. I don't know if this can be fixed.

"P-promise me you'll f-find him. Promise you'll get him somewhere s-safe."

"I promise, Mel. I swear." His eyes are wide with fear when he turns to me. "Get us out of here, Max, now!"

His words snap me out of my fog of adrenaline and fear. I grab both of their hands, and with everything I have in me, I take us to the only place I know that will help us. In the next second, we land in Ian's living room, shocking the shit out of Ian and Aidan as they stare open-mouthed, with game controllers in their hands.

In a blink, Ian's up and working on Melody, sending Aidan to get blood from a local hospital, doing everything he can for her.

But looking back, I shouldn't have taken Melody there.

I should have let Striker and Melody have their last moments.

I should have let him say goodbye to her. Because in the end, Ian can't save her.

No one can.

CHAPTER NINETEEN

STRIKER

There was a time in my life when I didn't think I could survive in the human world. Their emotions were too raw, too acute for someone who felt every single one of them but didn't have the same urgency of time. Time is what made those emotions so tangible, but time itself has always been a joke for me. I know I'll live an unending number of years, likely losing myself in the passing of them.

Melody was a bright spot of light in the dull, dreary days where I faked happiness because it was easier than answering questions. She was someone I could reach for— someone I could take care of. Max didn't need me. Not in the business, not in her life. I pulled my weight, sure, but she took care of me more than I took care of her, save for a few scrapes here and there.

Melody needed me. Me. Not Max, not someone else. I knew it the second she stepped into the shop. I saw the curve of her cheek and the light in her eyes and the swell of her belly, and I knew she was mine to keep safe. Instantly I hated the man she was with. Hated him more than I could possibly hate a complete stranger who'd never done me wrong.

In the scant minutes I had talking to her while Max was inking a fresh tattoo, I recognized the light in her. It warmed me when I'd been cold for so long, and I knew I would die to keep her safe.

So, when I climb the stairs searching for her and the baby, my brain can't process what I see. I flip straight to denial.

That can't be my woman. That can't be her blood soaking her T-shirt and the pale bedding underneath her. That can't be.

My brain can't process, but my body knows the truth when a howl of the fiercest pain rips up my throat and out of my mouth. I'm frozen in the doorway, but not for long. Max grabs a hold of me, yanking me out of her way, and at first, it's a good thing because I can't get my body to move, even though I want to kill Micah.

This isn't happening. Not to her. I refuse to believe it. She's not dead. My sweet Melody isn't dead. No.

I pull myself together, willing my legs to move, to bring me closer to her.

"M-my b-baby. He t-took my baby." She shudders, her sweet voice slurred and distorted by blood loss and shock. Her once-tan skin is gray and clammy as she shivers, reaching for my hand. I give it to her, feeling her fragile fingers in mine.

"P-promise me you'll f-find him. Promise you'll get him somewhere s-safe," she begs on a panting breath, her pale-blue eyes boring their way into my soul. Of course I'll find her son. If it's the last thing I do on this planet, I'll find him.

"I promise, Mel. I swear." I reassure her the best I can. Her body seems to wilt further into the mattress as her eyes turn glassy.

I scream for Max to get us out of there, and she takes us to Ian. Ian, to his credit, jumps in to help, sending Aidan to get blood, Max passing him instruments and supplies as he works on Melody. Somehow, I'm shoved out of the way— either as a result of my own inaction or on purpose, so I don't have to see just what they are doing to the woman I love.

But I want to see what they are doing to her. I want to know if her eyes ever open, or if she's in pain, or if she's breathing. I want to know if the ultimate dread I feel will ever go away.

But a minute later when Aidan comes back, Ian is giving her compressions, and Max is pumping oxygen into her mouth with a bag, and I'm still just standing there, motionless, because I cannot fathom a world where this beautiful, wonderful woman isn't alive.

Soon, everyone stops. They stop compressions, and Max stops squeezing that stupid bag, and Aidan stops hooking up her IV with his filched O-negative. They just stop because Melody isn't breathing, and she won't start anytime soon.

I push them out of my way so I can see her. Her skin is so lifeless, so gray. Her lips no longer the blushing rose I loved so much. A tiny smudge of blood dots her cheek, so faint it could probably be a freckle. And it's that tiny little nothing smudge that drives me over the edge.

Crawling up on that pool table that served as Ian's surgery slab, I wrap Melody up in my arms, her lifeless limbs dragging against the felt as I pull her to me. Pressing my lips to her forehead, she seems so cold already, and the grief finally hits me. I can't handle the wrenching in my chest that tells me she's really gone.

But this can't be how this ends. There has to be a way, there has to be some way to bring her back. Melody was carrying a half-demon, maybe she can come back like Max does. Maybe...

"Take me to Caim's." My voice is a guttural form of

agony ripping up my throat, but that doesn't matter right now. What matters is getting Melody to someone who can help her.

Max just stares at me, her eyes filling and spilling over as she shakes her head no, matted blue whips of hair shaking with it. There's blood smeared on her cheek, and it kills me that it's there.

"I'm not taking you there, babe." Her voice is trembling as she denies me.

"Yes, you are."

"No. I'm not. I know what you're thinking, and I don't want to know what Caim's price will be to bring her back. I'm not letting you do this to yourself, and I'm not letting you do this to her. She died, Strike. Humans die."

Anger pulses through me at her words. "And what would *you* know of death?"

"Not enough to say I've lost someone I've loved. I've never felt anything like what you feel for her, but that means I can see clearer than you can. I don't feel the same grief you feel, so my mind isn't clouded by it."

It would hurt less if she'd just stabbed me through the heart. I reluctantly lay Melody back down on the felt, careful not to disturb her body before I jump off of the pool table, getting right in Max's face.

"My mind is not clouded. Everything is perfectly fucking clear. Melody is gone because we couldn't protect her. She's gone because I was too slow to find her. Because we didn't find her in time. So, I'm going to fix this shit. And you are going to help me."

"You're right. It's our fault, but Striker, she's dead, and I'm not letting you lose yourself to Caim—whatever the hell he is—to bring her back," Max argues, and I swear everything in me seems to burst into flame with the rage coursing through my body.

I feel a strange ripping sensation at my back as the inferno under my skin reaches critical mass, then a heavy weight where there wasn't one before. Then a sharp bite on my palm, but right now, I don't give a shit about any of it. I only care about getting to Caim so he can fix this mess and bring Melody back.

Max's warm-brown eyes go wide, and she backs up a step, and then Ian's there in front of her, all fangs and talons and black eyes like I'm going to attack her. It burns that this is the third time in so many days where it's Ian in between me and my best friend. And what does that say about me, where a stranger looks at me like I'm going to hurt her?

"Striker, look at your hands." Fear laces through Max's voice as she peers around Ian.

Black talons have sprouted from my fingertips, and my hands seem to be coated in thick red scales like the hide of a lizard.

What the actual fuck?

"Umm, babe, I don't want to alarm you, but you have wings, too."

That explains the weight, but honestly, I don't give a shit if I stay like this, or if this is just some fever-dream hallucination brought on by grief.

"You're taking me to Caim." The guttural growl of my voice rips through the room. It's deeper, louder than what I'm used to hearing. But it doesn't really matter. The influence I've used almost every day of my life seems to be doing exactly dick to convince Max she should take me where I want to go.

"No, she isn't, but I will," Aidan offers, sidling up to us, getting in between his brother and me and farther from Max.

I back up, giving Aidan a nod and he grabs my upper arm, smoke surrounding us like a blanket as I feel like my body is being ripped apart. I land on my hands and knees on a plush Persian rug I've seen before. I have a hard time not puking all over it.

"What the hell, Aidan? Is this really necessary?" Caim complains. "What's th—" His voice stops like a record scratch when I climb to my feet and look him in the eyes. Caim's face turns gray for a second before he drops his gaze and gulps.

I must look pretty hideous if he won't even meet my eyes.

"I need a favor," I begin. "The woman you said you'd help us find? She's dead. I want you to bring her back."

"No." His response comes immediately, and it hits me like a blow. This was my shot, my one chance to bring her back and he won't even hear me.

"No negotiation? No questions? Just, no?" I ask in disbelief, denial rising in me by the second.

"I'm not in the business of resurrecting dead humans. So, again, no." His words are like a slap in the face. Caim has been trying to recruit me into his rather secretive business for ages.

"Please, I'm begging you. I'll give you anything. I'll do anything. Please." I'm begging, but I couldn't give a single fuck. Screw pride. Fuck everything but whatever will give me Melody back.

"You don't have anything I want, Striker. And if you need the explanation, resurrecting your Melody would take someone else's life, someone whose time has not yet come. It would screw with the Fates, and I make it a point to never mess with those women. It would be like telling my bosses to go fuck themselves. I choose to keep my head right where it is, thank you. I can't help you, son. No one can."

"I'm not your bloody son. I'm no one's son, remember?"

A blanket of rage settles over me, but instead of the frenetic fire racing over my skin, it makes my mind crystal clear. I know exactly what I'm going to do. If I can't bring Melody back, I'll for damn sure have the next best thing.

Micah's head on a fucking spike. Armistice or no, I'll have my revenge if it's the last thing I do.

CHAPTER TWENTY

MAX

I have no idea why I thought actually having a plan would work out for us. In my experience, having a plan meant utter and complete disappointment. I've had my plans dick me over, but never in all my years have they done so in quite such a fashion.

Melody is dead.

Striker is gone.

And I have no way to get Micah's blood to make the demon blade without killing myself in the process. I'm not just fucked.

I am *fucked*.

Not just that, but I failed this sweet girl. I failed her son. I failed her family. I failed Striker. And I'm about to become a demon's plaything to do with whatever he wishes. With the burning ache in my chest and pit in my stomach, I'm half-tempted to use the blade on myself.

Getting rip-roaring drunk seems like the best course of action.

"Please tell me you have alcohol in this frat house you call an apartment."

Ian turns, looking at me with an expression I can't read. His brow is furrowed, his eyes still the phased inky black, talons and fangs galore. I don't know why he doesn't phase back to normal, but I've got my own problems right now, and Ian isn't one of them.

"Why do you care so much for a man in love with another woman?" His question catches me off guard. He asks this like he has the right to know, which since he's put himself between Striker and me a couple of times now, I guess he might.

"He's my best friend. And we're not like that. Sure, he's hot, but Striker and I don't work together that way. I care about him because he's one of the few people on this planet who doesn't treat me like I'm a freak. Being Rogue is hard. No coven will accept me. I can't go to a lot of Ethereal places—can't be among my own kind. I can't shop at certain stores. And if someone hurts me, there is no one I can go to, and no one to help me. I'm fair game. Striker doesn't care about any of that. We've been watching each other's back for a while now."

Striker also never seemed to care what being friends with me did to his social standing. He was covenless too and just didn't give a shit.

"So, you're like family?" he asks, his phase bleeding right out of him.

If by family, he means we screwed once and hated it, so we decided platonic was the way to go? Then yeah. But I don't say this to him. There is no scenario where telling Ian I screwed Striker once in a fit of drunken misery is a good plan. Just no. Plus, there is this whole thing about it being none of his bloody business. But a tiny part of me wonders if that's true.

"Yeah, and right now he's with your brother probably asking Caim for something impossible, and Fates know what he'll offer as payment. I can't help him, and I can't get revenge, and I can't get these fucking brands off. I am well and truly screwed. Plus, I have a mountain of guilt piling on my soul and don't have the blood I need to avenge her. So, alcohol? That would be awesome right about now," I remind him, but he doesn't move to get me the sweet oblivion I need, the dick.

"What blood do you need? Show me the spell, maybe I can help." While his offer is nice, and it's cute that he thinks he can help, I'd rather be drowning in bourbon right about now.

Snottily, I pull out the folded parchment, pointing out

the ingredient in question. "It says 'blood of the demon's line.' Which means I could get it from Micah himself or his child. I don't have either, not that I'd take blood from a baby, so I'm pretty much shit out of luck."

Ian frowns at the ancient piece of parchment I pulled from my back pocket. Yeah, I probably should take better care of it, but it's not like a grimoire exactly goes with this outfit.

"Why don't you take the blood from Melody? The baby came from her—wouldn't that make her of Micah's line?"

Something inside me revolts at the idea of using Melody at all. Like I would be violating her in some way. It must show on my face because Ian's expression turns pitying.

"She's dead, Max. There's nothing you can do for her now except take down the bastard who did this."

He's right, I know he is, but my face still crumples, and my eyes still pour rivers of tears at the thought of using Melody in any way. Dammit, she's suffered enough. Taking from her now that she's gone seems... wrong somehow.

"It could work." My voice is clogged with shame, but I still wipe the wetness from my face. I don't have time to be a guilt-ridden whiner right now.

"You don't have to do it, Max. I'll draw some blood from her body with a syringe. We won't hurt her, okay?

Why don't you fix yourself a drink? I think there is some bourbon in the cabinet next to the fridge."

He's giving me an out, which I really freaking appreciate, and I take it, spinning away from the dead body on the pool table and the kindness I can't seem to absorb right now. Ian's kitchen overlooks the living and dining spaces, but I try to keep my eyes on their task of searching for booze. I find a bottle of bourbon in the designated cabinet, along with a tall tumbler and get to pouring.

But the burn of the alcohol only seems to make the hollow feeling in my chest worse. I should have looked for Melody before searching for the weapon. I shouldn't have wasted so much time looking for Striker and went off on my own to get her.

It makes me wonder if Melody and her family would still be alive right now if I just kept my nose out of it. But then I remember her words.

He's going to kill me as soon as I give birth.

No. I remember her fear, I remember her pain. If I'd have left Melody alone, there would be no one to find that child. Her parents didn't even know she was pregnant until we brought her home to them. There would be no one to avenge her. No one to stop him. And dammit, I'm going to do what I have to do to make sure he never does this to another woman again.

I take another swig of bourbon and set the glass down.

I need my wits about me if I'm going to outsmart that bastard.

"Okay, it's done," Ian calls, but I can't make myself turn around. Can't I take a nap? Or maybe go on vacation? Why is it me doing this and not someone else?

I mentally slap myself. Melody arrived on my doorstep. I said I'd help her, and that's what I'm going to do, dammit.

Put on your big girl panties and suck it up. No one is going to save you. No one is going to protect that child. Get it together.

My self-induced pep talk complete, I turn to Ian. My eyes catch on a white sheet covering Melody's body, and I can't help but be grateful he took that small bit of time he had to respect her body.

"What else do you need? I have supplies here..." He trails off, his eyes assessing in a way that makes me uncomfortable. I think that has always been my problem with Ian. He is forever looking at me like he's waiting for me to understand something, waiting for me to clue in on the joke.

But I can never seem to grasp this unspoken whatever it is between us, and I'm forever feeling like an idiot.

"You're going to do something stupid, aren't you?"

I shrug. "I think we've established that this whole plan is stupid, so, probably."

"No. I mean you are going to do something to get yourself killed."

I choose not to process his words, and instead, listen to his voice—reveling in the faintness of Ian's Irish accent. He still has a bit of a lilt to his words—or at least he does when he's pissed. Kinda like he is right now.

"Haven't you heard? I can't die." I state the obvious truth he knows all too well, still not meeting his gaze.

Then he's there in my face, so I have no other option but to look at him. His dark eyes assess me, and if I didn't know better, I'd say he knows what I'm going to do, even though the plan in my head has barely formed.

"You know what I mean, Max."

Something nags at my brain with him being this close. It's like I remember him from somewhere else but don't, all at the same time. It pisses me off, and so do his questions.

"I'll do what I have to, just like I've always done. And if that means dying, then it'd be par for the course. But I don't plan on getting myself killed if that's what you mean."

My answer is brash and filled with more bravado than I currently have in stock, but so what? What's that saying? Fake it till you make it? Well, I'm going to have to fake it all the way to the end on this one because I have serious doubts about the "making it" part.

Ian gives me his most dubious stare until I almost cave.

"Why don't we see if I can even make the damn blade before you go into protection mode? Okay?"

"Fine. We get the blade taken care of and then we can kill this asshole."

"What's this *we* shit? *We* aren't doing anything. *I'm* making the blade, and I'll take care of Micah. *You* are staying here and alive. Because only one of us can come back from the dead, and sweetie, that's not you."

"We'll see about that."

Is he high right now? No, honestly, is he? How many deaths does he expect me to have on my conscience? I take a few steps back, needing the clarity only space will provide.

"Ian, I can do many things with my abilities. Honestly, the possibilities are almost limitless. What I can't do, however, is worry about one more person that I care about getting hurt because of me. So, I can put you to sleep. I can paralyze you. I can make you think I never came here for help. Hell, I could make you forget you ever met me. Don't test me on this because the options are endless, and I don't think you'll like what I'll pick."

"I'm just supposed to stand here and let you run off to get yourself killed? As far as I know, you have zero hand-to-hand experience. What happens when you can't use your magic, Max?"

"That's what the blade is for."

"Are you kidding me?"

"Why do you even care?" I throw my hands up, exasperated with this whole conversation.

"I give a shit about you, Maxima." Ian growls in my space once again with fire in his eyes. He's so close I can feel the heat of him through my clothes. Something about the way he says those words makes me think he really means it. He cares about me. Funny, when he says my name like that, it doesn't make me cringe. It doesn't bring the hurt I've become so accustomed to feeling.

He gives a shit about me.

But why?

The question almost falls from my mouth when he moves closer, his body flush with mine. His hands find their way to my hips, pulling me, pressing me against him. I can't look up. If I look up into his eyes, if I stare into those fathomless brown pools, I'll kiss him. If I kiss him, something tells me I won't want to stop. Hell, I know I won't want to stop.

And I can't do this right now.

My body revolts, my heart thundering in my chest, my breath short little pants of want, but still, I manage to pull away.

"Okay," I concede, my voice like broken glass, "I'll make the blade, and then we'll make a plan."

"That, I'll agree to." Disappointment mixed with a bit of hurt laces his words. I don't want to hurt him, but I can't focus on it right now.

I can't abandon my promise.

"Then pass the blood so I can get cracking. This blade isn't going to make itself."

Step one: procure a way to kill Micah.

Step two: try not to die.

Step three: figure out what the fuck is going on with Ian.

Should be a piece of cake.

CHAPTER TWENTY-ONE

MAX

The spell to make the blade demon-ready is easy —a little too easy, if you ask me. Every step of this saga-of-shit has been awful, so I kind of thought the spell itself would be a significant pain in the ass.

It isn't. In fact, the Aramaic text even has the phonetic spelling written underneath it in Teresa's terse scrawl. I guess Mommy Dearest didn't want me to screw this up. In all honesty, this is probably the most helpful she's ever been in her entire life, so I'll take it.

I couldn't stay at Ian's—not with Melody there—so instead of wasting more time waiting on Striker and Aidan to do whatever it was that they felt they had to do, Ian took me to my shop. It's Monday so the shop is closed— not that I've even taken the time to think about my business or my employees since Micah steamrolled all over my life.

But someone has. The front window has been replaced in the few days I've been gone, and the walls and light fixtures have been repaired. There isn't a smell of fresh paint, so magic has to be the culprit. The room has a scent to it, the slight ozone of spent magic and the unique spice of the person who cast it.

"You fixed my shop, didn't you?" I turn to Ian, who is still frozen in the middle of my little waiting area, staring at the hand-painted mural I'd done ages ago on my walls. It's a blooming cherry blossom tree, the pinkish-white blossoms caught in a windstorm, floating off into the beyond. The walls are uncracked, the plaster smooth as a baby's butt, and the light fixtures that used to be reduced to shards of broken rubble are gleaming and intact once again.

"Striker said he'd called everyone and told them there'd been a break-in. Let them know to cancel their appointments for the next week so everything could be repaired. But no one was here to help you fix what was broken, so I thought I could."

He doesn't even know the half of it. But a part of me believes Ian could probably fix anything if he has a mind for it.

"Thank you." I manage to croak out, unable to meet

his eyes. Sure, my vision is a little wobbly from fresh tears, but I power through.

It's one of the nicest things anyone has ever done for me, and I decide that when this is all over, I'm attacking Ian Moran and kissing the shit out of him. Probably more than that, but I can't think about it right now.

That will have to wait until I do the damn spell. Oh, and kill the demon who branded me and murdered an innocent woman.

You know, no big.

"You're welcome," Ian says at my back, and the rough timbre of his voice does some things to me. Some floaty, girly, lusty things that I'm totally unprepared for. The sound of his voice pitched this way nags at my brain once again, but I can't place why.

Finally, I manage to unstick myself and coast to my office, spinning the dial on the handy-dandy magic-proof safe, and grab the carved bone blade my mother so reluctantly bestowed upon me. She was also reluctant to tell me exactly where the weapon came from, but I managed to pry a few details about it from her. She wouldn't say when it was created, but based on the thin leather wrap on the hilt, I'd go with a few decades past ancient. More than likely, it should be stained brown from age and use, but it remains pristine as if it were just carved from the humerus bone my mother said it came from. She wouldn't disclose who or what species provided it or if it was taken by force, and at this point, I'm lucky I don't know so I won't feel any guiltier than I already do.

I skirt past Ian and through the shop, up the back set of stairs to the apartment above, heading straight for my supplies and altar. Unfolding the parchment from its home in my back pocket, I go over it one more time.

I'll need a salt circle, the blood Melody's sacrifice provided, and the blade.

I have everything I need, but I can't seem to start. I hate to even think it, but I'm scared. So much more than I am pissed. But then I remember Melody's voice on the other end of the line whispering how scared she was.

She was brave when she had every reason not to be.

She was brave even though I failed her.

I can be brave, too.

Sucking it up, I set the blade in a large hammered bronze bowl, drawing a circle of salt on the wide-planked hardwood floor around it. I hold my hand out to Ian, and he places the thick syringe in my hand, filled to the brim with Melody's blood. Depressing the plunger, I douse the pristinely white tang in the lifeblood of my fallen friend.

We'll get him, baby girl. I promise. I'll get him for you.

Next come the chants in a language I don't understand. Aramaic hasn't been on my list of languages to learn, but I may need to start. I use the carefully crafted phonetic guide my mother provided, haltingly at first, but my words get clearer the more I say them. I immerse my fingers in the thick, red liquid, cupping my hands to pour the blood over and over the blade, careful not to nick my fingers on the surprisingly sharp edge.

A strange vibration starts pinging its way through me, almost making my words falter, but I power through, chanting the phrase over and over. Then, the bowl starts spinning, and I yank my hands back before the blade can cut me. The blood pooled in the bowl's depths seems to funnel into the blade, the bone sponging up the lifeblood as if it were dying of thirst. Candles that were not lit before, burst to life, their flames peaking high into the air before snuffing out altogether.

Snapping my fingers, they come to life again as I peer into the bowl. The blade sits there, pristine as ever, not a drop of blood left in the basin that holds it.

Well, that isn't creepy at all.

"I think it worked," I hesitantly say aloud, praying that somehow my words don't jinx me.

"Good. Now you have to find him. How did you do it the last time?"

I glance down at my bandaged forearms. I haven't looked at them uncovered since Bernadette abraded the flesh, too scared to know if my time was up.

"I followed the link to him from the brands he made on my arms."

Admitting that hurts somehow and I don't know why. Well, I do because without uncovering them, I already know that the burns are healed. I grasp the fact that my time is all but gone.

"So that's what they are." His voice is like glass over gravel. He might have suspected, but he didn't know. And now it is too late for me.

Too late because I know where he is. I know he's looking for me and I can feel it. A tiny siren's call tapping at my brain, begging for me to come to him.

"Yeah. But I don't need to follow the magic. I already know where he is."

This catches Ian by surprise, and his gaze on me turns sharp as a razor's edge.

"How do you know?" It isn't a question, more like a demand.

"The brands are healed, Ian. I'm too late." My voice cracks as I confess my death sentence—the awful thing I have tried so hard to prevent. I've failed at everything. Four hundred years on this planet, and what do I have to show for it?

"What do you mean, too late?" a voice calls from the stairwell, a voice I know all too well.

Striker moves into the wide-open room, his wings and

talons gone, but his wrath is still there in full force. Aidan is behind him, hanging back, and already the place is wired, the frisson of his rage pinging against my skin.

I don't like that I can feel Striker's emotions. It means that he is too out of control to harness them. Even if the phase he couldn't hold back is concealed under his skin, it roils underneath his flesh, just waiting to come out again —waiting for the rage in his blood to ignite once again.

I don't know what Striker really is. I don't think he does, either. But the violence finds its target when his eyes fall on the blade still sitting in the bowl on the floor.

I know if Striker gets the blade before I do, he'll start a war—a war I don't think either of us will survive.

I don't know who gets to the knife first, or why I feel the excruciating pull yanking us from that room, draining me. All I know is when Striker and I land on the still-warm pavement of a suburban sidewalk, we're no longer in my shop.

It takes a second before I recognize the turquoise door attached to the pretty white house, but once I do, I know exactly where we are and why we came.

This is my house, and without a doubt, Micah is behind that door.

And worse?

I don't have the blade. Striker does.

CHAPTER TWENTY-TWO

MAX

Looking at my house from the sidewalk, no one would ever know there was a demon lurking inside. I suppose that was the goal of the illusion charm, but the magic hiding my house doesn't work on me, and still, my pretty house with its wide wraparound porch and navy shutters call to me. Even though my skin, my brain, my bones know that Micah is inside, I still want to follow Striker in through my front door.

I still want to trail behind my best friend and go inside. Well, I do, and I don't.

As much as I want to kill him for what he's done, want to run that blade deep in his gut, being this close to Micah is beginning to seem like a mistake. My wrath is muted, my thoughts wrapped in the fluffy cotton swaddling of the brand's magic.

It has to be the brand, right?

I want to go inside even though I no longer have a weapon, even though my magic seems to have been dulled, but there is a part of my brain that's screaming. It's a woman's voice that sounds so much like mine, but it gets farther and farther away, drowned out by a sudden lethargic pall that makes me want to go inside and lay my head down on my pillow.

Yes. That's it. I'm tired, and I want to go to bed.

The heat of the sidewalk scores at my fingers as I struggle to stand, but then my hand brushes cool metal, and I manage to focus for a slant second. A pale-blue stone winks at me from the pavement, glittering from the streetlight.

It's pretty, so pretty.

As soon as my fingers close around the ring, the fog from the brand burns away. The ring Bernadette gave me must have slipped off during the struggle over the blade, and Micah is using his control to try and trick me.

The dick. Both of them.

Shit! Striker has the blade, and if I had a guess, he's already in the house. I can't see him from my inelegant crouch on the sidewalk, but I'm not as dumb as I look. I have mixed feelings on this. On the one hand, Micah is in there, I don't have the blade anymore, and I'm pretty sure he just tried to mind-fuck me. On the other, if I don't stop Striker from killing him, he'll violate some ancient treaty and start a war. I think.

Somehow, I think out of everyone, I'm going to be the person who gets screwed over in this scenario.

The more my mind comes back, the more I know I didn't bring us here. I just wanted the blade, and to keep Striker from doing something stupid. And if I didn't take us here, that means Striker used me. He used my power as if it were his own. I feel as if he must have siphoned off some of my energy, and that knowledge feels like a hard slap when I'm already knocked down. That must be one of his tricks that he's kept from me.

It hurts that I've been used so callously by someone I trusted. Someone who has been vital to me for so long.

I have to go into the house. I know I do, but there is no way I'm walking in the front freaking door like Striker did. Instead, I make the likely idiotic decision to snap my fingers, arriving in my living room. It looks exactly the same as it did a few days ago.

Was it days? It feels like a lifetime since everything got turned upside down. I decorated this house and every single room in it. I painted those walls the brilliant peacock blue. I picked the slate-gray couch and every single goldenrod, plum, and teal throw pillow. I chose the plush area rug and the funky but cute art on the walls. I made this house my home, and while nothing seems out of place, it feels like a stranger's. It doesn't feel like mine anymore, and I hate that the home I spent so long creating for myself seems lost to me.

It almost feels as if I've been robbed.

But haven't I?

Deciding to find Striker before he screws us both over, I try and sense where Micah is. If his earlier mind-control taunts are any indication, my bedroom is a solid guess. I have to suppress a shudder as I try to gauge where Striker could be. After this long together, I should be able to feel him, right? I should be able to sense where he is using whatever demon juju is locked inside me, shouldn't I?

The faint whimper of a baby crying has me turning my ear to it. I can't tell if it's coming from the door that leads to the basement den and casting room or the dreaded flight upstairs where I know Micah is.

I close my eyes, trying to isolate the sound, knowing I'll go for Melody's son long before I try to save Striker. Striker is older than me, and he's armed. The baby isn't. Plus, the baby is innocent in all of this. If I see Striker, I'm punching him right in the balls first and then getting his dumb ass out of here.

Even in the back of my brain, I get that he's running on

rage and not using his head, but shit, can't he just stop and think for one Fate's forsaken second?

I don't get an answer to my question because a rough hand closes over my mouth as a strong arm clamps around my stomach from behind. I can tell by the tattoos and combination of height and muscles behind me that this isn't Striker. Oh, and the general putrid 'I'm screwed and not in a good way' feeling I've got going on.

Without warning, Micah snaps us from the living room, popping into my bedroom without a second to spare. My stomach pitches, and I deduce demon traveling is no better than wraith traveling.

"I said I'd come back for you and look at that, you've come for me instead." Micah's thick British accent presses into my ears, inciting a body-wracking shudder.

It doesn't help that his lips—which I want nowhere near me—brush the shell of my ear as he says it. I don't want to be in his arms. I don't want to be this close to a bed. I don't want this man to keep breathing.

"Oh, come now, pet. I'm not that bad." His voice is honey on gravel, but he doesn't fool me.

"Tell that to Melody." I seethe, gritting my teeth as he tightens his hold.

"Melody was human. Simply a host for my seed." He rubs his lips along the column of my neck. I used to find that attractive in a man. A man could kiss me there, and I'd become pliable. When Micah does it, my stomach roils. "You, on the other hand, are much different. Practically royalty, you are. But no one protected you, did they? Let you be named Rogue so any demon could snatch you up and make you theirs. As long as you've been around, I figure it's a damn miracle you haven't been claimed by now."

"I don't know what you're talking about."

"Don't you know who your family is, love? Your father, the demon Andras, only son of our High Queen Lilith. You know her as Bernadette."

"You're saying that Bernadette is my grandmother?"

"Yep. I'd recognize this ring anywhere." He snatches up my right hand to get a better look at the ring that saved my mind. "If you looked at the sigils, you'd know what family you belong to. Spells it out good and proper. Why do you think I want you? What better trophy to have than the granddaughter of the High Queen and daughter of the Crown Prince?"

"So that's what this is? I'm a trophy. I guess it doesn't matter to you that I'd rather burn at the stake again than be your pet?" I growl, testing the hold he has on me as I try to yank away.

Unfortunately, I don't get anywhere but held tighter. Shit.

"It's 'cause I can't get into your head, if I could you'd be begging me to take you."

"Aww, did I hurt your fragile little ego? You can't mind-control me, so you decide kidnapping and enslavement is a good option?"

Micah's talons grip my chin, slicing into the fragile skin just under my jaw as he cinches his arm tighter around my waist. His actions tell me I may have struck a nerve. Whoops.

"You think a challenge will best me? No, pet, I'll take this ring off you, and you'll do exactly what I want you to do. I'll complete your branding, and no one will be able to take you away from me. Not even your high queen granny."

I hope he's not lying—that the brand isn't complete. That I'm not his—at least not yet.

But then I can't hope for much of anything at all because even though I struggle, even though I yank and stomp and kick, Micah rips that ring off my finger, damn near breaking it in the trying.

I feel his influence almost immediately, the cotton-candy fog of it clouding my mind. My limbs relax, my fear fizzles out, but with it, goes my sense.

"Come now, pet, let me see your brands."

The smart part of my brain is screaming for me to run, to snatch that ring back, to shout for Striker. Fucking anything but sit here in Micah's arms and let him mind-control me into slavery. But I don't, and the longer I stall, the more I forget why I'm worried about Micah in the first place.

I reach for the white surgical tape that holds the gauze to the healed brands, when a baby's cry sounds through the room. The woman in my head, her screams are getting louder.

Melody's son is in this room. You promised to help him, to keep him away from Micah.

You promised, you promised, you promised.

Micah's grip is lax, so this time when I yank, I manage to get free.

But only for a second.

In the next, my hair is wrenched, bringing my head back and clotheslining me faster than I can blink.

"You think I'm going to let you go that easy, pet?" His voice is a coy sort of whisper that makes the pit in my stomach grow wider, blooming into pure dread.

Then Striker's in the doorway of my bedroom, his phase a shining beacon of hope that fizzles out when he doesn't move to help. His fiery eyes glaze over as Striker stands stock-still, immobile, except for the breathing.

Micah's sudden laugh brings gooseflesh to my arms and a chill down my spine. It's a joyous kind of sound, and coming from him, it's a harbinger of pure fucking evil.

"Oh, how adorable. He thought he could save you both."

That's when I know. Striker can't help me.

He can't even save himself.

CHAPTER TWENTY-THREE

STRIKER

I screwed up. I know I have, but getting out of the mess I made is going to hurt more than just me.

I shouldn't have gone to find Max in her shop. I shouldn't have fought her for the demon blade. I shouldn't have siphoned her energy, making her take us to wherever Micah was.

I shouldn't have, but I did.

Blinded by the rage that courses through my body, I dicked over the one person who has never left me behind. My need for revenge had me leaving my best friend in all the world, dazed and drained on a sidewalk where I knew Micah could get to her.

The cry of Melody's son echoes through the house, a siren's call slapping me in the face with all the wrong I've done. All the vengeance in the world won't bring her back, it won't let breath and life flow through her. She won't grow old, watching her son grow up. She won't be with me.

Killing Micah won't do anything but snuff out another life. While that is appealing on so many levels, somehow, I still seem to lose.

Melody's son cries again, the baleful whimper of a hungry child, and instead of looking for Micah, I change direction, searching for the child instead. The staircase to Max's room never seemed so steep as it does right now, each stair taking me closer to the child I'm afraid to fail.

My hand trembles as I push open Max's bedroom door, my phase rippling over my flesh before the wood even leaves the doorjamb. But what I see isn't what I thought I would.

Melody is sitting up in the middle of Max's bed, her back against the tufted headboard, her son in her arms as she pats his diapered bottom trying to soothe him. At first, my heart can't take the sheer joy I feel. I must have dreamed her dying, or maybe she came back like Max does. Maybe it was the worst nightmare I could have, the vision of her bloody and gray, the life running out of her body one faltering heartbeat at a time.

My legs can barely hold me as I stagger to the side of the bed.

"M-Mel? Baby?" I can barely speak as my hands find

her face, cupping her cheeks as I press my grateful lips to hers. I can't believe it. The thought she could come back was always a pipe dream in my head. A part of me never really believed she could come back at all, but having her sitting on this bed when I thought she was gone forever is the only wish my soul could ever ask for.

"Isn't he beautiful?" She smiles, and then her eyes fall back to her son as she runs a fingertip over the line of his cheeks. I follow her gaze, memorizing the way her fingers graze the line of her son's flesh, the way she holds him, the way she protects him. I could watch her forever.

"You holding him is the most beautiful thing I've ever seen." My voice breaks, still unable to get myself under control. The love on her face. Fates, I never thought I'd see her again. Never thought the crevasse left in my heart would ever heal. I've never been more grateful for anything in my entire life.

We sit in silence for a few minutes before a niggle of doubt hits me. I want to know what happened to her. I want to know if she's really okay.

How did she get here? How did she find her son? Why didn't she come to me?

"Baby, what happened to you?"

"I died, Striker," she says simply, but her voice, her tone is wrong.

"But you're here now. How did you get here?" As soon

as I ask the question, dread filters back into my chest. She sounds like an echo, a copy.

"I don't know, you tell me." She continues to stare at her son, content in her own ignorance.

Or maybe it's something else. This is wrong. This feels wrong.

I look up at the sun streaming through the window, filtering through Max's curtains and highlighting the soft beauty in Melody's cheeks. But her face is a little too full. Her nose a little too rounded. Her lips a little too wide.

I don't want to pick this blessing apart, but...

It was night when I got to Max's house, but it's day now.

Did I miss the sun coming up?

No. I don't think I did.

"Melody, baby, can you look at me?" My voice is pleading, and when her eyes meet mine, I know, the clawing ache of loss hitting me all at once.

My Melody died yesterday. She bled out on Ian's pool table after a barbaric cesarean. She was left to die after she served her purpose. She was used and discarded as if someone that beautiful, that precious was disposable. My Melody was sweet and sassy and wonderful. She didn't accuse, and she didn't blame.

But most importantly, unlike this Melody, my Melody had blue eyes. They were the very first thing I noticed about her when she walked into the shop—the pale icy blue of them a stark contrast to her dark hair and tan skin. I looked into her wide eyes, and I was lost.

This isn't real. None of it.

And it's like I've lost her all over again.

Keeping the piercing agony off my face is almost impossible. My greatest wish, everything I would have bargained or stolen for, is crumbling to dust and I have to sit here and smile.

Because I'm going to get out of this trap, and I'm going to take Micah down.

If it's the last bloody thing I do.

MAX

"Let's complete that brand, shall we?" Micah murmurs, more to himself than to me. His influence on my mind is heavy, a thick leash of evil making my body do exactly what he wants it to do.

Unfortunately for him, the baby makes a plaintive cry again, and it clears my head some. Trying to catch him by surprise, I elbow Micah in the gut, yanking away from his hold.

But I don't run. Not this time. I already know running won't work. He has my ring, and without it, he can find me anywhere on this tiny little planet.

What I need is a distraction, a way to incapacitate him long enough for me to either get my ring back or search Striker for the damn blade and cut his stupid murdering head off. I would pick door number two, but it's a question of time at this point.

I try my first spell, muttering the Latin phrase I've used several times in my past as a method of interrogation. *"Mille vulnere."* *One thousand cuts.* Micah just smiles at me. My spell does nothing. Not even a paper cut this time.

I try another. *"Flumine sanguinis."* *River of blood.* This one isn't one I've used much. One, because it is freaking disgusting, and two because it's a shitty way to die and I'm not fond of killing people—at least people who don't deserve it.

Nothing.

Again.

"River of blood? Pulling out the big guns on that one, aren't you? Sorry, pet. Those spells won't work on me. Not anymore." He smiles venomously, his hand latching onto my forearm faster than my eye can track.

"None of your spells will work on me. Don't you get it? I own you." Micah's lips curl around the words like a lecherous caress. His power presses in on me, nearly taking away my will again as he shoves me against the wall, caging me in.

The more I fight him, the more pissed off he gets.

Then, both of his burning hands latch onto my forearms. While there are plenty of shitty memories he could make me see, I know his game and I fight back, forcing him out of my mind, his own head rocking back as if I'd slapped him.

"You don't own shit."

The shock on Micah's face is so precious, if I had a camera, I would've stopped to take a picture.

"You bitch! You think you can keep me out? You think you can say no to me? No one says no to me, pet," Micah growls, his eyes glowing red, fangs peeking from beneath his lips.

Then, it's me who is shocked. Micah's face twists in fury as his power washes over me, flooding my body with his influence, with his fire. But something is different this time. Either Micah has flexed a little too much muscle, or I'm finally getting some mileage out of the half-breed demon status.

I'm drowning in his power, my mind clear for the first time since this mess started. I feel the energy pulsing out of him and into me. I'm draining him. Not on purpose or with any conscious thought on my part. No. It's him. He's trying to bend my mind to his so much he's flooding me with everything he has.

So much, he's losing his hold on everything else. Over Micah's shoulder, I watch as Striker comes back to himself, his body slowly becoming less frozen, his eyes focusing on the room instead of what was inside his head. I don't know what he saw, but whatever it was is enough to have my heart burning in agony just in response to the expression on his face. He's more than wounded. Whatever has cut into his soul was made of the worst sort of poison.

Striker is silent as he draws the demon blade from his belt, stepping toward us like a ghost. I never realized before just how quiet Striker can be, just how lethal. The furrow of his brow, the set to his lips, the wrath on his face, I wonder not for the first time if I really know my best friend at all.

I can't help the tendril of fear that steals through me as he comes closer, sidling behind Micah without so much as a whisper.

When the blade finds a home in the meat of Micah's shoulder, I don't expect the blinding agony that rips through my body. I really don't expect the warm wetness of blood pouring from my own shoulder. Micah staggers away from me, his talons scrabbling at the wound in his shoulder. If I could move, I'm sure I'd be doing the same, but all I can do is slide down the wall that can't seem to hold me up, landing with a jarring thump on my hardwood bedroom floor.

The room tilts on its axis as I try to pull in a breath. I

didn't know it would hurt this bad. I didn't think killing Micah would be the end of me.

But I think it might be.

Striker drops the blade, skirting around Micah and pressing his hand on my shoulder to staunch the flow of blood weeping from the wound. His touch only makes me cry out, unable to hold the agony of it inside me for one more second.

I know what I have to do. It can't be Striker who kills Micah. I can't let my best friend in the world start a war when I won't be here to help him fight. And I won't be here. I've already figured that much out for myself. If a cut on Micah does this to me, what will killing him do?

I'm not stupid. I know if Micah lives, he'll kill me or Striker, or worse, sell off that baby to the highest bidder to do Fates know what. He won't stop until he gets his trophy. I don't know what my family did to Micah to make him hate us so much. If my demon side is anything like my witch side, I can see where making enemies isn't exactly a new thing.

But it's a debt I'll pay if it means my best friend gets to live. I'll pay it if it means no war. I'll pay it if it means I finally get to keep my promise to a young pregnant girl who never even asked me for help.

I'm saving her son. I'm saving her love.

And I'll get vengeance on the man who stole her life out from under her.

I tilt, pulling away from Striker and sliding closer to Micah. The blade is close, but the white-hot agony ripping through my shoulder make three feet seem like a mile. Striker tries to stop me, but I think he's more worried about hurting me more, so his touch is gentle.

By the time I get to the blade, Striker's already figured out what I'm going to do.

"No, Max. No. We'll find another way."

"Th-there isn't another way, Strike. He'll just keep co-coming. He'll just t-try again," I stutter, my fingers closing around the wrapped leather hilt.

"No. Please don't."

Micah jerks pitifully, trying to scrabble away, but at this point I'm half-lying on top of him to reach the bone knife, the sharp double-edged blade coated in his blood. Then I feel the barest inkling of his power trying to filter back into him.

He's trying to escape. Not if I can help it. Tightening my grip, I heft the knife that seemed so small an hour ago into my hand.

"Love you, Strike," I whisper, trying to convey all of my remorse for what I'm about to do. I'm leaving him. I promised I wouldn't do that to him. I promised so long ago that I wouldn't abandon him the way everyone else had.

At the time, I didn't think dying was an option, so it was an easy promise to make. Now, breaking that promise is just as easy.

As the blade pierces Micah's chest, Striker's scream is the last thing I hear.

CHAPTER TWENTY-FOUR

MAX

A man's voice filters in my ears, calling me from the blackness that has swaddled me in silence for far too long. He's singing softly in a tune I can't place, but the song doesn't matter, the light that seems to seep through my eyelids does. Forcing them open, it takes a minute for the room to come into focus.

Softly lit by a bedside lamp, Ian's bedroom feels familiar and comforting after clawing my way back from the dark. My eyes drift to the side, falling on worn jeans and a pair of rather attractive bare feet crossed at the ankles.

"Maxima? Baby?" Ian's voice is a pleasant mix of surprised and relieved, but the words themselves trip a hair trigger in me I didn't know I had.

"Why do you call me that?" I snap, not really meaning

to, but my full name plus the endearment grates the shit out of my nerves.

"Maxima or baby?" Ian's tone is neutral. He doesn't sound hurt, but his face tells another tale.

"Both."

"Well, I call you Maxima because you're a chick and Max is a dude's name, and I call you baby because I'm totally and completely enamored by you, and it's my subtle way of showing it." Ian's wry answer makes me chuckle.

"So noted, but no endearments, please. No baby or honey or darling. Just don't, okay?"

After Micah, I'm not sure I can handle another man calling me anything other than Max.

"You wake up after two damn days, and it's 'don't call me honey'? Are you kidding me?" Striker gripes, and I whip my head to my right to see him sitting in a leather club chair with a burp cloth on his shoulder patting a diapered baby booty.

"Two days? That's… excessive." I don't think I've ever been out for more than a day.

"Excessive? That's all you're gonna say? Not 'sorry you had to watch me kill myself' or maybe 'sorry I played martyr for the seven thousandth time and got myself killed'? Jesus fuck, Max."

Striker's eyes flash gold. He's pissed, but he doesn't

have any right to be. I didn't take us to Micah. I didn't put us there at all.

I put a hand on the bed to shove myself up to sitting. Striker's aching for a fight, and I'm just pissed enough to give him one.

"Look, I'm not the one who put us in that situation in the first damn place. I'm not going to argue with you about what went down because I did what I had to do, just like I always do what I have to do. You don't like it? Don't go off half-cocked with a weapon that can start a war. Sound good?" I spit through gritted teeth, and it takes a second for me to realize that the shaking bout of rage I feel isn't just me, it's the whole damn room, probably the whole freaking building.

So my abilities have kicked it up a notch. Interesting.

Honestly, it's a giant slice of shit cake on top of a shitty couple of days. Why not add to the power I already can't seem to control? That won't backfire on me. No, surely not.

Worry pings in my brain for the first time since I woke up, and I scrabble to search my skin for the brands Micah left. Both arms are the smooth tattooed skin, the brand that had burned my skin just days ago missing. I run my fingertips over the skin, just to reassure myself that they are indeed gone.

Melody's son fusses a bit, drawing my eyes to the tense way Striker clings to him.

Oh, no. No.

"You can't keep him. You know that, right?" My words are harsh, but unfortunately, they are also true.

"Why the fuck not?" Striker snarls, both arms circling around the baby as he clutches him closer.

I don't want to be the bad guy here.

But the both of us made Melody a promise. We promised we would save her son. We promised we would get him away from Micah. We promised we would keep him safe.

Safe isn't with us.

"He isn't yours to keep. You aren't a demon. You don't know what his powers will be or what instruction he'll need. You have no idea how to raise him, nor are you equipped to do so. Look at me. Look at how I was raised. Do you think I would have been killed so many times if I knew what I could do or what I was capable of? Even you. You have no idea what you are. How can you raise a child when even you have no idea what you can do?"

Striker's eyes, which were filled with anger just a second ago, turn wounded. Jesus, I do not want to be the bad guy.

"But I'll love him, isn't that enough?"

"For some, love can conquer everything. But you can't

choose the course of a child's life based on just love. You need to be smart. You need to choose him instead of playing into your own grief. You can't keep him just because he's that last bit of Melody you have left." My tone is soft, but my words are barbed. There just isn't another way to say it, and it has to be said.

"Fuck you, Max. Fuck. You." Striker seethes because I'm about to take away the one thing that could dam his grief. I get it, but I shouldn't have to be on the receiving end of this horse shit.

"Fuck me? What happens when Micah's friends realize he's dead, hmm? Won't they come looking for us? How are you supposed to keep him safe then? Answer me. How?"

But Striker doesn't have an answer for me because the answer is, he can't.

WALKING INTO CAIM'S OFFICE WITH A NEWBORN in my arms goes over about as well as one would expect. After three days of wearing Striker down, I finally got him to see my side of things. Sure, the brands were gone, and Micah was dead, but I didn't trust that we were safe.

I couldn't let Melody's son pay the price if I was right.

"What the hell are you doing here?" Ruby demands, "And what the hell is that?"

I ignore her. For someone who tried to help me stay alive and out of slavery, she sure is surprised I'm here. I don't think Ruby and I will be braiding each other's hair anytime soon.

Instead of giving Ruby the time of day, I lock eyes with Caim. "I would like to speak to you without an audience." I keep my voice as bored as I can make it. Letting either of them know just how much I need them seems like a bad plan. Caim and Ruby feel like predators to me now, and I don't understand why. If I show either of them the least bit of weakness, I have an inkling they could smell it. I wouldn't be here at all if I could avoid it, but Caim owes me a favor.

Caim's lips quirk just so, a subtle upturn of the mouth so quick Ruby misses it. "It's fine, Ruby. Leave us."

I hate to admit, but I get a sick sort of satisfaction out of her stomping off in a huff. Yeah, no. We're never going to be besties.

"Your problem has been taken care of, which means you owe me a favor and I'm here to collect."

"I owe you, huh? And how is that?"

"Without me, you would never know about Micah running a black-market site right under your nose, and now that he has been handled, you won't start a war. Sounds to me like you owe me big." My words are blunt and to the point.

Caim assesses me for a minute, steepling his fingers as he looks the baby and me over. Melody's son fusses for a second, so I drop the diaper bag on my shoulder and start rocking him. All things considered, he is probably easy for a newborn, but I haven't gotten the hang of him yet. Readjusting his pacifier and cooing at him for a bit seems to do the trick, and he settles back down. I think he looks like Melody with his pale-blue eyes and light-brown hair that will no doubt darken with age, and somehow it gives me comfort to know a piece of her lives on.

"What is this favor?"

"I want you to find him a good home. A place where they are kind, and safe, and won't eat him or make him feel like shit for being half-human. I want him to be brought up knowing what he is and how to use his powers. I want him loved. You have in your possession every single registered Ethereal, right? Find someone on that list who wants a baby who can train him and love him. You do that, and I'll call us square." It's a big ask, I know, but I killed a damn demon and almost died to prevent an all-out war. A big ask is par for the freaking course around here.

Caim's forehead furrows in confusion and he sits just staring at me for a moment, while I adjust my little bundle so he's sleeping on my chest. I wish I could give him a name, but it just doesn't feel right. He's not mine, and he's not Striker's. We don't get to bless him with something so precious.

"You could ask me for anything, literally anything, and with what you've done for me I'd have to help you, and you pick helping this boy over any amount of riches or power you could possess?" Disbelief is clear in Caim's tone.

"I made a promise to Melody that I'd keep her son safe. I keep my word, Caim. Always." And I don't make promises I don't keep, I want to say, but I don't. Who knows what he promised my mother—or didn't promise her for all I know? Out of the two of them, so far, Caim hasn't dicked me over, so I'll take his word over hers at the moment.

"You are nothing like your father." The statement catches me by surprise. I don't know Andras, but I do know Teresa. If I'm nothing like my mother and nothing like my father, who the hell am I like?

A question for the ages, I bet.

"You know him? Is he a bad man?" I ask the child-like question slipping out of my mouth before I can stop it.

"The worst. But he's a good man, too, just in his own way."

Well, that clears everything right up.

"You're better off not knowing, Maxima. Trust that at least."

"I'm pretty sure he's known where I was for the last four hundred years. I don't think he has any plans to get to know me, so I'll take your word for it."

"Good. Now give me the child. I know exactly who to give him to." He rises to his feet, pushing away from the desk and holding out his hands for Melody's son.

I give his forehead a gentle kiss, muttering a blessing for him that I hope will take before handing him over.

"Does he have a name?" Caim adjusts the little bundle in his arms with practiced ease. This isn't the first child Caim's held, not by a long shot.

"It didn't feel right to name him. Striker wanted to call him Ronan, but…" I trail off, shrugging. "It didn't feel like my place."

"I like Ronan." Caim coos to the baby, running a single finger down his chubby baby cheek. I've done that a time or two over the last couple of days, fighting with myself to not get attached to something so precious.

"You'll make sure he's safe, right?"

"Of course, Maxima. Children are to be protected." Caim's eyes meet mine for the first time since I handed the baby over.

His words give me a little comfort as I leave them to it, the aching loss I feel lessening just a bit.

Goodbye, Melody. I hope you are at peace.

"Again!" Aidan shouts, and I can't help but groan from my flat-on-my-ass position on the awful blue mat.

Fuck training, fuck bokkens, just fuck them all.

"You were the one who came to me to learn how to fight, Max. No one forced you, now get your ass up and do it again."

Who thought Aidan as my trainer would be a good idea? Oh, right, this girl.

Peeling myself off the mat, I question my sanity for the hundredth time.

"You do realize I could crush you with a snap of my fingers, right?"

Aidan just raises an eyebrow at me, not breaking a sweat, even though he's wearing a beanie.

Still.

In August.

I sometimes wonder what's underneath. Does he have a bald spot? A random growth? I may make it my mission to check one of these days. After my body quits hurting from the beat downs I've been getting.

"You realize that having a guardian train you is about as good as it gets, right? Magic doesn't always work. You can't rely on it. Isn't that what you told me when you asked me to train you?"

"Yeah." I sigh, snatching up the stupid wooden katana that has been the bane of my existence for the last three weeks.

"You're a natural, Max, probably one of the quickest studies I've ever seen. But you're lazy as hell. Now get into a fighting stance and let's go."

One of these days I'm going to kick his ass.

Probably won't be today, though.

AFTER OUR SESSION—AND A SHOWER—I HAUL MY tired ass back to the shop. Ever since the ordeal with Micah, I can't seem to make myself go back to my house in the burbs, so the apartment over my tattoo shop is getting a fair amount of use.

It feels weird now, coming into work without Striker

here. He tried to come back after everything. He did, but I could tell it was killing him. He'd look at the counter separating the waiting area and the rest of the shop, and the sadness would just wash over him. Everything in this place reminded him of Melody. Hell, I probably did, too. So, one day I let him off the hook.

"You don't have to be here, you know." A brilliant opener, but it was what I had to work with. Striker didn't have to be here. He was immortal (probably) with enough money to last until the end of time. He didn't have to be stuck with me in Denver. He didn't have to be in this shop with me, and he didn't have to be reminded every day of the love he lost.

"My name's on the deed right next to yours, Max. Of course I have to be here." His lifeless tone was killing me.

"You're going to let a piece of paper tell you how to live your life? You're miserable, and your sadness is killing me. How the hell are you supposed to heal if you're reminded of her every single second of the day?" I asked, mostly because I wanted to know.

I had the resolution of giving Ronan up to Caim. I had the closure of fulfilling Melody's dying wish. Striker never really had that. He wouldn't even let Melody have a funeral. I ended up calling Aurelia to help me inter her. No one knows more about funeral rites more than a phoenix, and given that my other best friend was a pile of depressed shit, I needed the help.

"I don't think I'll heal from this, Max. Melody wasn't a girl you just get over." His voice was hoarse with the pain he had shoved deep down inside.

He was probably right.

"But you're right about one thing, I don't have to be here." He nodded to himself before walking across the shop to brush a kiss on my forehead, sparing me the hug, even though I would've probably accepted one from him.

He left without another word, and in the last few weeks, I haven't heard from him. As much as I know it's for the best, I really hate it. Striker and I haven't gone more than a week without talking to each other in a century, so the distance sucks hairy monkey balls.

Letting myself into the back entrance, I climb the staircase, my sore legs crying with every step. I hate being sore. I loathe sweating. But the confidence of knowing I can take care of myself is something I can't quite pass up. I need to know what I can do without powers, without magic. I need to be able to defend myself if...

For some reason, a tear falls down my cheek. It's been happening a lot lately, stupid random bouts of crying. I hate it. I feel so weak when I just start leaking out of the blue. But I get why it's happening.

One of my besties is off on his own. My house is probably going to have to be sold because I can't even look at the front fucking door without having a panic attack. Melody's dead and her son is gone—off to live with a couple who hopefully loves him.

But I can't stand to be touched since I've woken up, and I can't really sleep at night. I'm trying so hard to get my life back together, but it's like overfilling a paper bag.

The bottom always falls out eventually.

I park my butt in the middle of the staircase, delaying the inevitable lesson with Ian just a little so I can get myself under control. Along with Aidan training me in hand-to-hand combat, Ian is going over the basics of being a witch. Sure, a lot of the lessons don't apply to me, but I like knowing all the things I should have been taught by my mother. Even if the lessons are mostly a ruse so I can get to know Ian a bit more.

I thought I would be able to just jump into a relationship—or at least sex—with Ian after everything was over, but the no-touching rule is screwing me over, and not in a good way. I just don't want to shudder if he touches me, and I can't seem to make that happen right now. At least with the lessons, I get to have him in my life. Even if they are about as chaste as a ninety-year-old nun. Ian doesn't seem to be going anywhere for the time being, so at least I have that.

I haul myself up, contemplating what I can cajole Ian into picking up for takeout as I slog up the rest of the stairs. Before I even get the key into the lock, I know there is someone here. The ward hexes are gone. I understand it isn't Ian because he knows better than to waltz into my home without asking.

Not after Micah. Not ever again.

"You broke into the wrong fucking home," I call into the dark. "Show yourself." This isn't a burglar, that's for damn sure.

I snap my fingers, igniting every candle and turning on every light. I won't attack if I don't have to, but I want to see what I'm working with. What I really want to know is how they broke my wards.

Ruby is lounging on one of my tufted armchairs, her legs crossed as she inspects her nails in a show of boredom.

Oh, good. I need this tonight.

"You about gave me a heart attack, Ruby. What the shit?" Dropping my purse on the console table behind my velvet peacock-blue couch, I wait for an answer.

Ruby rolls her eyes before finally looking at me. I'll give her credit, the woman is beautiful, but Jesus, I wish she wasn't so... mean. She reminds me of my mother, and Teresa Alcado is no one to emulate.

"How many times have you dropped into Caim's

without so much as a hello?" she accuses, and she's right. I've been a little lax in the manners department, but give a girl a little warning, why don't you?

"Popping into someone's home is rude. Lesson learned. Any other tidbits of wisdom you wish to impart before you tell me why the hell you broke into my home?"

"I'm here to bring you in."

That doesn't sound good.

"Bring me in where?"

"To the Council, Maxima. You broke the law. You have to be punished." Ruby doesn't look too broken up about this. Hell, if I had a guess she's probably smiling on the inside. She has got to be dicking with me.

"And what law was that?" I scoff, not impressed.

"You murdered your Master," she says simply as if I'm supposed to know what the hell she's talking about.

"As far as I know, I have no Master. Good talk, though. You know where the door is on your way out," I bite out sarcastically, skirting around the couch to the kitchen. This day calls for bourbon and some ice cream. I'll worry about dinner later.

"Micah Goode. Ring any bells? You killed him, and now you have to stand trial."

I'm glad I'm not looking at her when she says his name, and I think I manage not to show any outward sign of fear. I really do need bourbon. A whole bloody bottle of it.

I reach into the liquor cabinet for the bottle of amber liquid. "Really? Are you fucking with me?"

"Afraid not." Her tone doesn't say as much. She sounds like she's suppressing a snicker, the bitch.

"Well, Ruby, I don't know much about Micah Goode except for he isn't my Master," I declare, just barely avoiding lying through my fucking teeth. I've lived for four hundred years, so my poker face is spot on. "No brands, see?" I show her my forearms.

I don't know why the brands are gone or how they left my skin. Bernadette said they couldn't be removed, so the reasoning behind it doesn't make much sense to me. Maybe when Micah flooded me with his power, he messed with the branding somehow. I don't know.

"Be that as it may, you're coming with me, Maxima," Ruby orders, and I know I'm going with her whether I like it or not.

Because Ruby is an angel, and if everything they say about me is true, then I'm a demon. If I harm a hair on her little head, it will start a war—a war I damn near died to prevent once already.

I've already been burned at the stake.

How bad could it be?

Max's story will continue with
Daughter of Souls & Silence
Rogue Ethereal Book Two

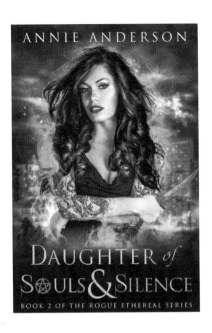

DAUGHTER OF SOULS & SILENCE
Rogue Ethereal Book Two

A Council full of Ethereal Elders wants me dead. Yep, it's a regular Tuesday.

When you kill a demon there are consequences.

Centuries-old witch, tattoo artist, half-demon... none of those titles are going to save me this time. The only way

I'm going to get out of my death sentence is to take down the biggest, baddest demon there is... *My father.*

And I thought being burned at the stake was bad...

Grab Daughter of Souls & Silence today!

THE PHOENIX RISING SERIES

an adult paranormal romance series by Annie Anderson

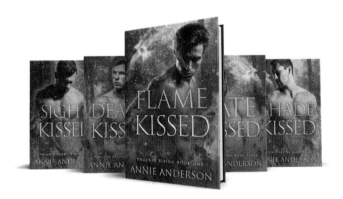

Heaven, Hell, and everything in between. Fall into the realm of Phoenixes and Wraiths who guard the gates of the beyond. That is, if they can survive that long...

Living forever isn't all it's cracked up to be.

Check out the Phoenix Rising Series today!

THE SHELTER ME SERIES

a Romantic Suspense series by Annie Anderson

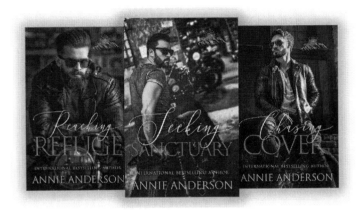

A girl on the run. A small town with a big secret.
Some sanctuaries aren't as safe as they appear...

Planning to escape her controlling boyfriend, Isla's getaway hits a snag when a pair of pink lines show up on a pregnancy test.

Levi just needs an accountant. Someone smart, dependable, and someone who won't blow town and leave him in the lurch. When a pretty but battered woman falls into his arms, he can't help but offer her the job. If only he can convince her to take it.

As an unexpected death rocks this small Colorado town, Isla can't help but wonder if her past somehow followed her to the one place she's felt at home.

Check out the Shelter Me Series today!

SEEK YOU FIND ME

A Romantic Suspense Newsletter Serial

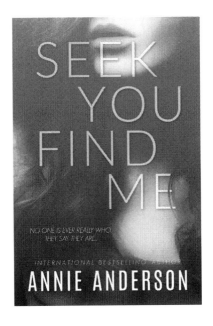

Never fall in love with your mark.

Gemini Perry knows her sister's accident didn't happen like the newspapers say. The truth has been buried and Gemini is just the woman to dig it up.

But the closer she gets to the man responsible for her sister's death, the blurrier the lines become.

Because someone wants the truth to stay dead, and they're willing to bury Gemini along with it.

Join the Legion newsletter to receive your monthly dose of SEEK YOU FIND ME.

www.annieande.com/seek-you-find-me

ARE YOU A MEMBER OF THE LEGION YET?

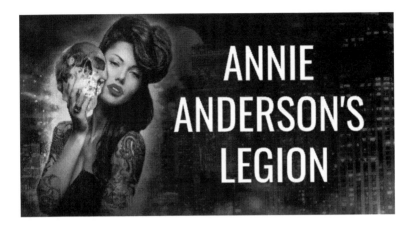

To stay up to date on all things Annie Anderson, get exclusive access to ARCs & giveaways, and be a member of a fun, positive, drama-free space, join The Legion!

facebook.com/groups/ThePhoenixLegion

ABOUT THE AUTHOR

Annie Anderson is a military wife and United States Air Force veteran. Originally from Dallas, Texas, she is a southern girl at heart, but has lived all over the US and abroad. As soon as the military stops moving her family around, she'll settle on a state, but for now she enjoys being a nomad with her husband, two daughters, and old man of a dog.

In her past lives, Annie has been a lifeguard, retail manager, dental lab technician, accountant, and now she writes fast-paced romantic thrillers with some serious heat.

Connect with Annie!
www.annieande.com

facebook.com/AuthorAnnieAnderson

twitter.com/AnnieAnde

instagram.com/AnnieAnde

amazon.com/author/annieande

bookbub.com/authors/annie-anderson

goodreads.com/AnnieAnde

pinterest.com/annieande

Made in the USA
Middletown, DE
15 July 2020

12696784R00146